THE OFFICIAL WIFE

OTHER BOOKS BY THE SAME AUTHOR

The Adventurous Sisters - 1993 (Children's Book)
The Curse of the Sacred Cow - 1994 (Play)
Child of A Delegate - 1997 (Novel)
The Invisible Weevil - 1998 (Novel)
Milking a Lioness and Other Stories - 1998 (Prose)
Blood Brothers - 2001 (Children's Book)
The Brave Hunter - 2001 (Children's Book)
The Man who ate his Eye - 2001 (Children's Book)

The Official Wife

Mary Karooro Okurut

Fountain Publishers

Fountain Publishers Ltd
P.O. Box 488
Kampala
Email: fountain@starcom.co.ug
Website: www:fountainpublishers.co.ug

First published 2003

ISBN 9970 02 401 9

Cover photograph: Eva Mbabazi of Ziper Models, Kampala

DEDICATION

To all those who count sheep;
may you find sleep.

APPRECIATION

A very big thank you to Gawaya Tegulle for tirelessly reading and making useful comments on the manuscript.

Also thanks to Violet Barungi, Barbara Kaija, Pat Haward, Samantha Sherurah and Ayeta Anne Wangusa for their wise counsel.

Special thanks to Mrs Joy Ibarah for always being there for me.

CONTENTS

CHAPTER ONE

INSOMNIA

It's way beyond three a.m in the morning – no, not morning, night. It is the *Bazungu*, our white friends, who call such an hour of the night morning. Such insolence to nature! For us in Africa, as long as it is still dark, then it is night. No argument there. And as long as the birds have not chirped out their morning greetings, as long as we cannot see beyond our noses and as long as there is no sign yet of the sun, then it is still night. Us here, we religiously adhere to the scriptures. As in Genesis 1.3:

> 'And God said, let there be light, and there was light.
> ... And He separated the light from the darkness. And God called the **light day** and the **darkness** He called **night**.'

But for our brothers and sisters from across, this whole thing of night (time), which they call morning, is a scandal to say the least. How can anybody in their right senses refer to three o'clock in the *middle* of the night as morning? *Morning*?

For Christ's sake! Let's get serious. Three o'clock is the darkest hour of the night. It is also the hour when it is reputed that wizards get out and get real busy. Night dancers too don their bizarre costumes and embark on their bizarre schedules – the grisly tasks of singing out corpses from their graves and eating them with a clear conscience.

Why at three? Because it is taken to be the *real* time of the night.

Even the way we count hours in Africa is rather odd, from the white man's point of view. The way *they* count hours is definitely odd to us. For us the day begins where it should: the first hour of daylight is our first hour of the day–*sawa emu*. Not the seventh hour (*sawa musanvu*), as the white men would have us believe. So by the time the sun retires to bed we are counting (not six o'clock) but the twelfth hour. Nothing wrong with that; that is how things should be. Daytime should have everything to do with daylight; as much as night should be associated with darkness. Why should someone mix the two, so that the day begins at seven? Sounds *sus*picious.

God! Three a.m. (*p.m.* in my mental make up) and I haven't had a single wink! I keep on turning and turning in this hugely obscene bed: from one corner to the other like a small ship on a troubled and turbulent sea. More often than not, my feet get entangled in this maze of sheets and blankets and this sends me into a maddening rage much more than what the devil felt when he went to Jesus' tomb and found his presumed prisoner had escaped.

I can assure you freeing my feet from this maze is nothing to write home about. Tomorrow, I will make sure I bring one of the single beds into this room. Time to take courage and end this double bed mockery.

Double bed, my nail! The last time it was used by the two people who are supposed to be its tenants was during the *el nino* rains. You remember that time when the heavens opened up and relentlessly bathed blessed Mother Earth like it was the last opportunity forever? An unceasing furiously destructive torrent that threw open graves and washed out the coffins, only to transport them at breakneck speed and hurl them in deep valleys, thereby burying them under the rubble from massive landslides. Graveyard relocation, if you please. What else should we call it?

Mother Nature, please spare us! We are wreaking enough disasters on ourselves as it is and we always look up to you for healing.

Please, do not cause us to die twice like charcoal.

You know this thing of charcoal: they burn wood to get it.

Then after getting it, it is again subjected to a second burning when it is used for cooking, dying in the process and becoming ash.

That's not too unlike what the Bible means when it talks about the second death. First, you die. How you die depends largely on which continent you are on and how much you earn. If you are the average African, you will most probably die of snakebite, marasmus, beri beri, malaria, hunger or poverty. Or AIDS. Or all the above.

Yes, AIDS. In the Western World people there can afford AIDS drugs, that make them live on and on. In those countries, one is no longer on death row when AIDS strikes. Free drugs or at a token fee that they do not even notice.

Not like most of us, poor Africans, for whom AIDS is an immediate death sentence because we can't afford these drugs. The years many of us Africans spend with the disease – before it finally finishes us off with a mighty hurrah – are worse than years prisoners spend on death row. Even if you feed on chips and chicken every day, the fact that you are on death row makes all that taste like chicken droppings.

Oh that we had the technology to manufacture these drugs! Do not get surprised, though, if our friends in the developed world are getting the ingredients from our numerous forests. In the same way that they buy cotton or coffee from us, process it and bring it back and sell it to us at more than 100 percent profit for themselves.

I am not one of those who blames them for all our ills. For why can't we make finished products ourselves and export them? But we prefer to whine about unemployment when we are busy giving away jobs to them, as they process our products and go into serious industrialisation...

Somebody said that even if the cure for AIDS is found to be one glass of clean water per day, many Africans suffering from the abominable disease would still die from it. For how many of the so called people's representatives take it upon themselves to provide clean water for their people let alone educate them on how to purify the water they have?

You could even die of *bubonic plague*! Now that is one disease that afflicted the world centuries ago. But for Africa, diseases make an exception to the rule. However extinct they may be, nothing stops them from showing up once in a while just to make life even more miserable for Africans, punishing them for their continued existence.

And of course there is the Guinea worm – one that is drunk in water through negligence. Even if you only use a handkerchief to filter the water, you will survive the eggs of the Guinea worm. If you are unfortunate and you get the damn worm, eventually it will find its way out of your body through the skin, *bit* by bit. The wiser village folk have mastered the art of dealing with this impudent worm. As it emerges, they roll each bit that comes out on a stick. Gradually, over a few weeks, it will all come out, nicely rolled like spaghetti. Any simple or slight mistake that breaks the worm before it has fully come out will climax in the death of the person. If you tell the villagers to filter the water before they drink it, they will wail and whine that they are too poor to afford the cloth for filtering. If you tell them to boil it, they will tell you how firewood is hard to come by.

The wise villagers will prefer to wait several weeks, rolling the worm out with meticulous care, doing nothing profitable all the while. It won't be a strange sight to walk into a village one fine morning–just what the farmer prayed for–and find the entire population not in the garden weeding what promises to be a bumper crop, but on the verandahs of their mud and wattle pretences of residences.

There is one commendable aspect about these residences though –they are really neat inside. True, the blankets are too short (so one has to curl himself up like a foetus), the beds too narrow (so the feet stick out) and the whole concept of bedsheets exists only in their dreams. But at least there is some order around the little shacks. Not like some executive bedrooms where you find the shoes and plates all over the huge bed. And the dirty designer underwear of the master of the house comfortably tacked under the mattress.

The floors are swept clean and you won't find grass around the huts. It is not that they don't like grass around the homestead. It is only that the average man has three or four wives. So if he spent the night with wife number two, in the morning he will move around his other wives' huts to check for any strange footsteps – the compound is swept clean every evening. If he finds any footprints he does not recognise, then the unfortunate wench will go through fire explaining whom she spent the night with.

I was talking about the Guinea worm extraction.

In various postures – some buttocks up, others legs stretched – Guinea worm victims are undergoing treatment in typical village style. Around them, bent in honest concentration over their 'patients', the 'doctors', are busy rolling the Guinea worms around small sticks. The worms, not exactly enthusiastic about being rid of their fine habitat, are rather slow about coming out but are in diverse stages of doing so. It is hard to remain in one place when one end of you is being gently but firmly dragged out of the place you have so happily occupied for so long.

Curious at creatures being pulled out of the adults' bodies, several little kids are gathered around each treatment joint, providing running commentary as only children can on the proceedings. The quieter among them are providing commentary, but of a completely different type – a silent summation of the goings-on relayed with their eyes. As each segment of the worm comes out, the little eyes grow wider and a keen observer will notice that the lower lip also drops a little more. You don't have to be too close to the patient to know when the operation has been concluded. When the eyes – now the size of tennis balls – look like they will pop out at any moment, and you notice the flies that have been left free to run in and out of the open mouth (now as wide as a church door), you know another long and *unwilling* tenant has been evicted.

Then these good people will have the guts to complain of poverty, yet they spent the season evicting worms!

Then there are those who are infested with jiggers and spend precious time removing the vermin from their bodies. And then you find a whole Member of Parliament appealing to *donors* to supply his constituents with cement otherwise they will all be finished by the jiggers! The perpetual begging basket. My grandfather will tell you that all it takes to get rid of the vermin is to smear the floor with a mixture of sand and cowdung. Talk about free, abundant, organic products!

So if you are a true African you may die of all of the above – diseases, *not* of ignorance but infinite knowledge. Yeah, infinite knowledge. In some places it is taboo to use a pit latrine lest your kids die young or the women get barren. Now, not that they have flushing toilets by any means. No sir. The bush sorts out their problems with Nature's calls. So each time you walk down the path, you are likely to see somebody squatting by the wayside, willing out all the refuse in their body. But you will only see them if you are looking about you.

And a good idea too, this looking about you, especially since you are more than likely to step on a landmine or two – mounds of shit all over the place, just waiting to make your life miserable, either by ensuring that you smell like a sewage filter or your feet itching and swelling so bad everybody will say you stepped in a can of worms.

In Africa we do not need these so-called modern methods of family planning. This business of subjecting a woman to swallowing unpalatable pills or those lousy withdrawal methods.

No sir. We keep our families small by killing off some of the surplus kids, usually in a comical attempt to remove the 'false teeth' a.k.a. *ebinnyo,* that attack infants.

Strange though, why the false teeth choose infants of peasants and other illiterate communities, while ignoring those of the educated parents.

A high temperature, vomiting and severe diarrhoea will follow the false teeth and before long you have a dying child on you. No need to take the kid to the doctor – why waste all that money?

Take it straight to the witchdoctor, who with airs of authority and know-it-all written all over him, opens its mouth, examines the swollen gums and solemnly announces that they have false teeth. If I do not extract them, he assures you, this kid will surely die.

He skilfully sharpens a bicycle spoke on a grinding stone with a finesse that tells you he does this all the time. No need to sterilize the instrument; it has no germs. Germs cannot survive here, he assures you.

Forcing open the kid's mouth he proceeds to *dig* out the false teeth. There are of course, no anaesthetics here and the screams from the kid would break a seasoned executioner's heart.

Not this executioner, thank you. He goes about his business as though he is administering ice cream or peanuts to the little fellow who is now on the verge of fainting.

The blood gushing out would make Dracula fall in love at first sight.

'There; the maggots are out,' the executioner beams, expecting you to beam back, slap his back or pump his hand and tell him what a great doctor he is.

On a small banana leaf beside him are three rubbery pieces of flesh; presumably the offending intruders.

The mother is grateful and extracts some crumpled note from her bra, which she puts in the doctors' hand.

But the surgeon takes no offence at the aesthetics of the note; he only pauses to examine its appearance, confirm the value, smile back as he pockets it and then proceeds to bid you goodbye.

'Make sure you do not take the child to a modern doctor,' he cautions gravely, like one advising the rabbit not to wander off into the bush again, lest the wild dogs make a meal of it. 'Don't mix the treatments or else the kid will die.'

This is no time to argue. She nods agreement and takes the kid home. After two days it dies of some infection, probably tetanus or worse.

One kid less, the society remains. No population boom, thank you very much.

Of course you can't really blame these village folk. Their leaders (political hawkers, many of them) are so good to them come election time when they want votes. They buy them salt and sugar and this and that. No word, though, about how to improve their health. What for anyway? These chaps were just created for the use of the more privileged. Just there to provide the votes, not much use else.

So in Africa, death has been liberalised rather too liberally; we have end*less* opportunities to meet our Creator. That is why you hardly hear of suicides the way it is in the developed world. You don't really have to kill yourself in Africa, there are more than abundant opportunities to die, just waiting around the corner.

If you are in the Western World, that means you have a bit of money *on* you or *around* you. What this really means is that you don't die like the Africans who die like dogs, in ignominy par excellence. No sir. You will die of those rich men's diseases or if you like, the more *developed* diseases born out of obesity because of overfeeding on good food, the preserve of the developed world.

Good food like those deep-fried chicken reeking of oil from every pore, nicely done sirloin steaks, medium-done frog legs or snail steak that drips fat all round. Then you have all the kids literally blown out of proportion; at eight years the kid looks fifteen and is the perfect pig. His blood pressure is high enough to send all the doctors scooting to the emergency ward just to take a look. You get the feeling that all it takes to bring the tummy back into shape would be to pierce the tummy with a sharp object and after a small explosion that manages to rock the passing cars, the balloon will be no more. The best treatment for this kind of oversized kid would be to bring it to Africa, take it to those good old folks in the village who'd feed him on katunkuma - those tiny and bitter garden balls - and steamed bananas for a month or so. Give him plenty of boiled beans and millet bread. Of course there is nothing like ice cream, milkshake or chocolate (a very important and unfortunate aspect of the menu in the western world) as dessert among the village folks. What for, anyway? Simply chew a sugarcane after each meal and dessert is done. Besides, the teeth will stay clean and strong. Soon he will be as slim as a celery stick and stuff like high blood pressure will become a thing of the past.

True to form, just like they colonised us because they truly were dying to help this Dark Continent to 'see the light', in the same manner, because they like and feel for us, they want us to eat the *very* same good food. They are out-competing themselves to bring their manner of feeding to Africa. So now we their grateful recipients are also outdoing ourselves to show we are better off than our neighbours by spending a fine chunk of our earnings feeding like broilers or fine looking swine. So on a good day like when a man in the village sells his coffee, he comes home laden with a gallon of cooking oil and two kilos of beef, most of it immersed in layers of fat (it's all more fat than beef actually, that's the best beef – *enyama ensava)*. The wife commences to do a fine job of frying it – there is more oil than water in the pot. Now that *is* good cooking, because it ensures the family will put on weight – a sign of prosperity around here. So after eating like that they belch richly and declare – in between farts – that the usual African foods like millet should be banned! Next time you want to eat some good amount of oil, just visit one of these families when their *bwana mkubwa* has got his pockets going real good.

The people who have really embraced this good cooking are largely those women who live in the rows of one-roomed quarters called *mizigo* in trading centres. In the evenings they take out their charcoal stoves and sit on the verandah, each beside her door; armed with a cup - or can – of cooking oil and onions, tomatoes and meat. It had better be meat or your fellow women will dismiss you as broke. Or that your hubby is undergoing financial castration.

They are competing to see who can fry better. The one who does it best is the one with the largest amount of cooking oil. At the end of the day people eat more oil than food, sending their stomachs into terrific olympics.

I will support any foreign investor who calls for the ban of indigenous African foods and beverages; for indeed why should a mother give her child fresh orange or passion fruit juice when there is a Coca-Cola shop around the corner? After all, isn't Coca-Cola the soft drink of the developed world?

Why should an African wife in a progressive family bend in the shamba to pick green vegetables or eat just boiled beans when she can enjoy deep-fried foods? Stuff like beans and greens are foods for the backward and lesser mortals. Ought to be banned, I daresay! The serious Africans should eat food like spaghetti which is now all over the place, though I suggest special classes should be held for our people on how to roll it round the fork before dispatching it to the stomach.

* * *

I groan and turn and turn around helplessly in this stupidly huge bed. If I get the opportunity to remarry (you never give up hoping, you know, since I know a few cases who married after 90. After all, it is the body which ages, not the heart. Feelings are ageless.) I will make sure a double bed does not enter my bedroom.

But still this remarrying thing is mere wishful thinking on my part. Truth be told, I do not have the courage to do it let alone get out of this hollow meaningless marriage. Believe you me, it does take a lot of courage for an African woman to call it quits when the whole thing has lost meaning. As for me, my middle name is Coward. And for once this is spelt in all capitals. Mrs. Elizabeth (Liz) *COWARD* Ishaka. But mind you, only coward as in being unable to walk away from this empty relationship. But more of this, later.

It is only people like the woman Vice-President (names withheld *without* request) of a certain country who took courage and called it quits when she realised that her marriage was not going places. Her husband's idea of having a good time was beating her senseless and then gloating big-time over his accomplishments. After all, he apparently reasoned, how much better can fun get than when you are walloping the VP? How many men can ever have this privilege? By his count he had set a record of being the first man in Africa to beat a VP. Like an African typical and true, he seemed to be of the persuasion that the cat would not jump out of the bag; after all, *ebyomunju tebitotolwa* – what happens in the home should never be told to outsiders.

But the wife had certainly never appreciated this particular sense of privacy and belted out the truth to the entire nation. Those women who regard themselves as progressive cheered her honesty and courage, saying that it was a crucial step towards emancipation of women in oppressive marriages. That if a whole VP could talk, the doors were now wide open for lesser women to speak out – or even walk out.

The VP should have been awarded an honorary doctorate for her sheer and straightforward honesty. Many women in the women's movement are victims of domestic violence themselves–whether physical or psychological – to the extent that they would be qualified to add a chapter each to the finest book on the matter. But they advise their rural counterparts to walk out of abusive marriages, while they themselves cling to theirs. At least the VP *practised* whatever she preached.

The majority of men (who else?) and the more conservative women jeered and argued that *amaka gamanywa embeba* (it's only the rats which should know what is happening in the home; nobody else). In any case, they said, this was simply an excuse for women who thought themselves too good for their husbands, now that they had attained high position, to snub their men; she is setting a bad example in bad manners – now we shall have rebellion in every home.

The good VP declared the man had slapped her twice. Then there followed this chorus from male chauvinists:

'Slapped her twice? *Only*?'

"How can a whole man be reduced to opening for his wife every night, be she VP or whatever?' They went on.

When some people took the man on, asking him why he was beating the VP, he replied that as far as he was concerned he was not beating the VP, he was disciplining his *wife*!

Interesting. A man will not discpline – where discpline means the cane or the slap – his twenty – something year old daughter because she is an adult. But he will turn the said cane and slap on his forty plus wife! Obviously, adulthood shifts goalposts depending on what needs to be done by the master.

Just like my dear Ishaka who shifts goalposts from time to time. Ishaka has no problem telling his friends what I look like *down south* and how pleasant or how deep my well is compared to his other exploits, when he gathers with 'the boys' for an evening sip around the *malwa* pot.

But when I say anything that makes him feel not-too-manly, he opens his granary of proverbs and promptly issues three or four just to put me where he says is where women belong. How convenient! I mean about quoting proverbs and all. Culture comes in handy, *very* handy, when a woman needs to be put into her place.

I *hate* and *despise* men who discuss the sex performance of their bedmates. There is this tribe in my country who have specialised in this despicable art – that of discussing their mates' sexual distinctions, or usually, the lack of them.

The men of this tribe think the best lay is the one who switches on a tap of water during sex, in degrees that brings to mind Noah's flood. So they will rumble on and on about how this woman is good because she makes River Nile look like a small stream while the other is lousy because the Sahara desert couldn't be drier.

They put their women on too much tension. The poor females are so eager to be awarded high marks on how much liquid they can produce that instead of concentrating on enjoying the act, they are wondering how much fluid will come out. In the process, because they are so tensed up, they dry up and end up making fools – and failures of themselves. In a society where everybody has to 'make the grade' in everything, including the most sacred practice, the poor girls end up feeling real failures.

But again, come to think of it, suppose he is bragging about how great a lay I am, and giving me such a high rating, surely that wouldn't be too bad, would it?

After all, everybody – man or woman – does mind about what their mates think of their sexual prowess, if any, anyway. Who doesn't love to be told that they are the greatest lay in the land? Who, before, during and after each performance, is not waiting to hear those reassuring remarks that none does it better?

And for many a woman, when he says your pot yields better meal than your rival's, that is it! She won't really care too much which other mortar his pestle will pound in; the assurance that she beats them all is the ultimate fulfilment.

* * *

I was talking about this double bed thing. When the couple is using a single bed, they have no choice but to lie close together. Not too bad an idea in these rather cold times in the otherwise usually warm climes.

But this double bed affair is the ultimate in keeping couples apart! It gives the uninterested party an opportunity to keep as far away from the partner as he/she possibly can. They actually just fall short of falling off the bed. When one of the partners develops love allergy against the other, the situation gets so bad that even the thought of toes *accidentally* touching becomes a dreaded nightmare.

In short, ladies and gentlemen, the formula for giving presents to a couple is very simple and straightforward. Single beds are the best thing you can give a honeymooning couple. A huge double bed is wholly unnecessary, unless you are giving it to *four* newly wed couples.

No surprise here. Each couple will cuddle and cling so close that there will be no distance between them. As in *zero* distance. The outside eye will come to the conclusion that it is simply beholding one person whose rural appetite and generous helpings from the food cans have done him absolutely no harm.

No couple will realise they are actually sharing the bed with three other couples. Get an acrobat to do cartwheels on the bed, get a mason to break all the walls down and take off the roof; none will notice.

But don't you worry; there will be time for a double bed. When they celebrate their 10th anniversaries (in the unlikely event they ever get that far, especially in the so-called first world), a double bed will be perfectly in order – for each couple this time. None will notice the other all night long, for the simple reason that they will be miles apart. If they ever give each other attention, it will be the kind you'd expect Old Dog Tom to give Dr. Cat.

Double bed means *double problems*. Yes. Double problems. Take it from me. I am now a consultant in this field. A real one at that, not these fake so-called consultants that are now roaming everywhere.

Consultant in *this*, consultant in *that*. And the *other* one too and... Big, long and winding titles that actually mean nothing. *World* Bank consultant on *African* culture. Born and bred in Washington D.C, has never left America and has even no intention of setting foot in Africa. Give me a break! My grandmother would be the best consultant in this matter, never mind that her shadow never darkened a classroom door.

I must admit, though, that there is something I enjoy about sleeping alone: I can pass gas as frequently as I want and also as loudly as I want. And there will be nobody to raise a ruckus about it, enough to bring the house down. With me now, sleeping alone gives me space to do it – especially, *mental* space. Freedom of expression, if you see what I mean. As in *loud* expression. But when you are sleeping with a hubby with whom things have gone wrong, all the time you are uncomfortably trying hard not to fart. Even though it is natural to do it, something turns your stomach into a rumbling and rickety train fumbling on rusty rails. That is, if you don't do it.

His Excellency Ishaka always turns away in disgust every time a small fart accidentally escapes from my anus. And then I have to pretend I did not do it. Even though I know I am wallowing in self-deception. For when there are only two of you in the room, what is the point of denying the obvious?

Don't think he doesn't get involved in this act of denial himself. He always does after one of his thick silent farts. Then as soon as the stench assails the air, he turns on his most disgusted, judgmental look. But I always let go of my verbal artillery at such moments.

'Look here, do not give me that condemnatory shitty look of yours. There are only two of us in the room and since I obviously didn't do it, then it is you.'

He barks at me – in a way that a dog would envy – to go to the toilet whenever I feel like letting out.

Hmm! As if that is what he ever does himself. I mean as if he ever goes to the toilet himself whenever he wants to fart. Here is somebody who is always ripping off the father of all farts. What comes out of him would make the sewer smell like a sweet perfume. Actually with Ishaka there is no need to buy a gas canister. All you have to do is connect a cooker to his anus and you'll cook the driest beans in record time.

What makes me even sicker is that here is somebody who enjoys the smell of his own fart!

More than once, I have caught him actually putting his hand on his *gas pipe* as he gets ready to rip off this earthquake of a fart. I see the old hand slowly moving towards his anus. Then as soon as it is out, the foul air I mean, he kind of *scoops* it into his hand, closes the hand and proceeds to carry it to his nostrils.

Looking at him, you would think he is carrying some precious stone in his tightly clenched fist! A gem or somethin' for Christsake!

He then proceeds to open his *precious* gift close to his nostrils and begins to sniff at it sloooo-wly, obviously savouring every minute of his sick act.

God! How sickening. And all this while his Excellency rests assured that I am not aware of his sick act. I close my eyes and feign deep sleep while throwing in an occasional deep snore...

I was telling you about his reaction whenever a small one escapes me.

You would think the third World War has just erupted. Or that he has just seen a dead man rise up and walk. He gets up from the bed, furiously throwing off the covers and looking every inch like a wounded hippo emerging from the waters. Frothing at the mouth and mouthing unprintable obscenities, he screams for all to hear: 'How many times do I have to tell you that every time you want to let loose your sewage pipe, you should go to the toilet?'

Believe you me, he first throws the door wide open before screaming out this terrible accusation. All aimed at belittling me in front of the domestic workers.

I wonder why he does not purchase a Public Address System since his main interest is obviously to announce anything that belittles me to whom it may concern (twimc). Nobody should miss a single bit of the action, eh Mr. Ishaka?

Which worker, after hearing this sort of thing, will respect you? No wonder that I get the kind of reaction I do from my H.B.

H.B. is my abbreviation for houseboy. I never want to use the title of houseboy/housegirl. I think it is demeaning, dehumanising. So I call the houseboy H.B. Not like those Asians who call their houseboys *Boi*. Even when the H.B. is fifty plus and is old enough to be their father, these insolent Asians will still call him *Boi!* How insultingly annoying!

A man is the agemate of your father and you call him *Boi!* Just because you happen to have more money than he does is no excuse for giving him the same respect you give to your domestic canine which happens to be just some silly-looking mangy cur.

But it is not only the Asians. We suffer the same sin, for by calling the domestic workers housegirl/ houseboy we are also at fault.

I was telling you about the time my H. B. Gives me a stinker of a reaction.

I ask him, my H.B., to bring me a glass of water. He brings it. Jesus! Is he stinking! He is a mixture of the he-goat smell and urine of yesterday. I turn to him in utter disgust:

'Water here is free. You don't pay for it. We do. And so is soap. I mean it is free. So what in the name of thunder stops you from taking a bath? You either go and take a bath or you lose your job this very minute. One compost pit is enough without having to add on the one that your body now is,' I literally spit at him.

He looks me up and down and says in this very *despising* quiet voice that leaves me completely frozen: 'Why don't you first clean up your sewage pipe act?'

I can only open my mouth and it remains agape for some time, no words coming out. My brain has suddenly taken leave and I am momentarily stunned. With cynical courtesy, the houseboy – sorry, H.B. – calmly closes my mouth for me. A good thing he does too. Otherwise I am sure I would have lost count of the myriad flies that would have found their way there. Especially those huge green flies I detest more than anything in the world. We have so many of them around these parts, you'd be forgiven for thinking, after witnessing one of their noisy gatherings around one of the mounds of dog shit in our compound, that this is a global fly congress in session.

And as he does this, I swear he is smiling. One of those thick, oily smiles that tell you more than words that you are an imbecile, born and bred.

Did I apologise for calling him houseboy and revert to the more polite abbreviation of H.B? No. I should not have apologised. In fact in moments like these, I revert to calling him houseboy. For when he is so insolent and so insulting, that's precisely what he is: a houseboy. Or housegirl. Why should he deserve any respect?

Indeed at moments like this, I am inclined to remember the saying of our people: 'When you get too familiar with a dog, it starts calling you its *mukko'* (in-law).

I had always refused to be sucked in by the philosophy behind this saying that you should never put yourself on an equal footing with those who are below you. Thing is, it is ridden with snobbery. Something like 'familiarity breeding contempt'. When it is a dog, yes. But here, we are talking about human beings, not dogs! There is also this group that passes a blanket condemnation on these H.G.s and H.B.s. That they all went to the *same* school as far as their behaviour is concerned. Did the H.G.s and H.B.s. The school for malice or something along *those* lines. And graduated with first class honours degrees in dishonesty and hypocrisy.

Anyway, that saying of familiarising with a dog and all and its calling you its *mukko* has some moments of truth. For truly, I have treated this H.B. well. Buying him clothes, eating with him the same food on the same table and so on and so forth.

That's how I always treat all my domestic workers. But they end up stabbing me in the back.

Like this girl whom I had always taken as a younger sister. I thought she liked me too. Until the day I come back home and find she has scrammed. She leaves me this note:

Diya Mama Kirabo,

I amu very happinessi thata I amu leaving you for goods. (As though she had left me and gone to earn goods.)

You izi vere badi personi especially.(Funny how long some people take to learn a language as simple as English).

When you cames to married your husbandry, (!) *you were like me – no money, few clothings, no car.*

Nows, after many year, you have too much dress, you drives my car (popular reference to personal cars) *and you have builded house for your maaza*!

And me nothing. So I goes away to look for money also be rich like you for you have hyena heart you not make me rich like you.

But I am happiness about one thing only. Before I go, I making sure I punish you. I make you to eat my monthly blood.(What? Oh, my God! The English is horrible, the act much worse, simply horrendous.)

Yes, I get the blood from down **there** *and I put it in your tea and you drink and say aah, this tea very good. Then...*

I can't go on reading the devilish letter and I start retching. I vomit until I get scared that my internal organs will get torn into shreds. I keep on throwing up until there is nothing left to throw up apart from thick saliva. God, do I feel sick!

The little vixen! She has turned me into an instant vegetarian for any thought of meat will conjure up visions of dripping menstrual blood. Ugh!

When I am done with throwing up (if ever I can), I decide to read the rest of the letter. Maybe she has left a time bomb in the house. Better to find out before it explodes.

I first close my eyes and take a deep breath to prepare myself for further, sure shock.

And your son whom you takes like to be china cup, whom you thinks is everythings in world.

Yeeeeees, your presious Kirabo. And everytime you say I bathe him I am happiness because then I punishing you through him.

(Jesus! Am I sweating! At this rate I will drown in my very own sweat.)

I put him in water then I start to play with his ka thing. Then...

May the good Lord be with me. This is worse than eating the menst...puke... blood! Defiling my angel!

And yet here we are thinking its only girl children who are defiled! Then we never care to look out for boy-child defilers.

I can't finish the witch's letter. I contact the police who manage to trace and arrest her. I refuse to look at her otherwise I will resort to mob justice and gouge her eyes out.

I was telling you about this houseboy who told me *to my face* to go clean up my sewage act first. You will bear with me for I have this habit of digressing when I am telling a story.

That houseboy has to go. Not tomorrow or sometime. Today. NOW.

As I furiously throw him out of the house, I hear him murmur that people who live in glass houses should not throw stones!

All this humiliation is courtesy of his Excellency, my dear husband, Ishaka.

* * *

Nothing is more embarrassingly annoying than having a domestic worker who openly despises you. Ishaka has sealed my fate in that direction. For they all despise me. All the domestic workers, I mean.

And the housegirl. Sorry. Slip of the tongue. Remember the dictates of my heart? Can't call her housegirl.

I think of calling her the maid. No. Sounds too colonial. And makes me sound as if I am like on the same level with Her Majesty the Queen of England, if you please.

The maid. No. There is another reason for not calling her that. Reminds me of Joan of Arc – the young French girl who led an army against the British and defeated them. All agreed that she did come from God and that what she had done was a miracle. But the same bastards turned around and burnt the poor innocent girl! What was her crime after her heroic act of liberation: telling them the truth that exposed their hypocrisy, and ignorance.

Reminds me of this other man in some country who was put on firing squad. The poor fellow is seated in a bar sipping away at his beer with the composure of a cow chewing the cud. An argument soon erupts about the top leadership of the country. Our man shouts that the president of the country is a decidedly stupid man. He is whisked away by State agents. After the poor man is murdered, government is put to task by millions of enraged demonstrators.

'How can you kill an innocent man simply because he insulted the President when many other people are doing it?' Demanded the charged demonstrators.

'Insulting the President is not a crime. That man was killed because he disclosed a public secret,' the state answers. Same crime as that of Joan of Arc.

So although this girl is good by any standards, she is not made up of the stuff of saints. She therefore does not qualify to take on the title of the maid. So that's why I call her H.G.

She is a relative I brought from the village. A good girl. A decent girl. A *shamba* that has never been tilled; a bush that has never been explored, a virgin who intended to stay that way until she took the vows of marriage. She seems to have this *mortal* fear of men.

I swear she does. Whenever we get male visitors, she does not even want to enter the sitting room, for God's sake!

As for my husband, every time they chance to meet in the corridor or something, she seems to want to disappear into herself, I swear. You can see her practically coiling into herself, with the speed and airs of a millipede whose sojourn across the village path has been disturbed by nosy schoolboys poking a stick in its ribs.

'Why don't you tell this girl that I am just a human being like herself and she doesn't have to tremble every time she meets me? The way she goes on, you would think I am an ogre, for Christ's sake! Or one of the man eaters of Tsavo!' Ishaka says.

The man eaters of Tsavo is the title of a book that tells of these lions that devoured the men working on the East African railway.

Personally I have absolutely no problem with the H.G.'s *men-phobia*; as far as I am concerned that is a very useful sentiment in an H.G under the roof of a married woman. You don't want your man to go fishing in other waters, you don't want to catch him eating bananas in a plantation that ain't his. My joy in this regard is complete but I say none of this to my husband.

'Don't worry. She will outgrow it sooner or later,' I console him. I am telling him about her trembling fits born out of her fear of him.

She outgrows it *sooner* than later. Outgrows this fear, I mean.

For all of a sudden, she starts to change. Starts to imitate me in everything. Well, practically everything.

If I decide to eat with my fingers, she does the same. If I turn to the fork, she immediately switches to it. If I swing my behind this way she will soon be doing just the same.

There is a time I decide to change my entire wardrobe. I want to assert my Africanness and so I buy *bitenge*. These fabrics that have come to be taken as purely African wear.

After a few weeks, the H. G. approaches me: 'Madam, where can I buys *bitenge* from?'

I am a bit taken aback. '*Bitenge*? What *bitenge*?'

'Why, like the ones you are puts on nowadays,' she answers in this voice that clearly spells out that I have asked a damn stupid question.

Hmmm.

'Well, you can't afford the kind of *bitenge* I wear.'

She insists on putting on *bitenge*. When I pay her monthly salary, I take her downtown where there are cheap ones and she does her purchases. At this juncture, I am only irritated not annoyed.

Obviously, I have become her role model. A bit irritating the way she imitates me. But I shouldn't be the one to complain about the role model bit. Because you see, I would be contradicting myself. I am one of those in the women's movement who has been amplifying the importance of role models for the young girls. Except my H.G. seems to be taking the theme too far: I soon discover that she wants to role model me right to the bedroom!

Share with me the shock I get when I catch her in this role-modelling gimmick. She has gone to clean the master bedroom. I go there to pick up something. She is making the bed. As soon as I enter, she bends very low. In my vernacular, this is called '*Okukunamiriza*' – bending with the intention of exposing one's lower anatomy. That is what this girl does as soon as I enter the room. And oh great grandfather! She is not wearing any pant! Her rounded bums are as smooth as those of a blooming monkey. And I must admit she has a beautifully rounded small bum. Not like those bums that seem to stick out all over the place or the Indian type (forgive me, dear friends) that are as flat as a *chapati*.

It's not easy to find a girl with such a cute bum. I grudgingly give her bum an A+.

This bum thing is an issue in our culture. A very big issue. There are certain tribes who will not touch a woman unless she has a big, pronounced bum that sticks way out. In certain tribes, it is said that women go to the extent of putting a basin – *basin* for heaven's sake – on their bums before tying on the undergarments!

The story goes of how such a woman had the misfortune of the basin falling off while at a wedding reception. In a community where women are stopping at nothing just in order to make the grade in terms of beauty, no one begrudged her. They quietly applauded her creativity – as soon as they could cease the giggles.

Yet still other women are rumoured to tie rolls of sackcloth on their bums before putting on their swathing clothes.

So this girl is lucky to be the proud possessor of such a bum.

I can clearly see that she is *bending* intentionally. The H. G. I mean. Obviously, she cannot be trying to seduce me. This business of lesbianism – females letting loose their passions on each other as though there are no men who would be only too happy to do it for them – is not in our culture. Even this whole concept of gay men is just not in our culture, though some say that one or two of our many kings used to have their own men for supper.

My grandma says this is going against nature and this whole thing of going against nature is what is causing us problems. Around these parts of the globe, we used to shave our heads clean only when a close member of the family died. But these days, just because some film or football star has no hair on their head, the Africans follow suit. Although I try to convince her that culture is not static, she remains adamant in her views. 'Why provoke nature thus sorely?' She continues. So why should we complain when people around us are dying so casually, death has become a way of life in many communities?

Kwosiga emiriire yawe oraarakwo – if you abandon the way you eat, you go to bed hungry, grandma says.

In the old days when somebody died, people mourned passionately, donned sackcloth and rolled over and over. No food until the late is put in his final resting place. Nowadays we have chosen the opposite direction. The moment someone dies, we throw a party. We dress festively, and then bring out all the beer, chicken and meat. We fry the rice and steam-heat the *matooke* (green bananas). Our appetites exceed their usual limits as we sip and swallow with relish and gusto. Death has therefore taken a cue saying that, since we celebrate so much whenever he pays us a visit, since we get so happy and festive that we dress for him, cook for him and pamper him to the utmost, we have opened the door wide in his honour. He has indeed got the message and chosen to call in more frequently just to make sure the party goes on and on and…

Next thing we'll do, says grandma, is send out cards inviting people to attend a funeral like we hear happens in the land of the *bazungu*. Here when someone dies, people come naturally to commiserate with the bereaved. There is nothing like 'the family of so and so, with deep sorrow invites Mr. and Mrs. this or that to the funeral of their beloved...'.

* * *

Back to this H.G. that I found bending dangerously in the bedroom. *Very* dangerously. Her seductive bend could only have been targeting one person: Ishaka. Poor lecher. Thinks it is Ishaka who has entered the room. That is why she decides to *kukunamiriza*. Wrong number, you lustful wench.

I quickly get hold of the broom and give her such a violent swat across her bottom I fear she will not sit on it for a week. Certainly a walloping she will not forget in a hurry.

As she hollers, she says between sobs, 'I'm sorry, Mummy.'

'I'm sorry Mummy, my arse! Just get your butt out of here.'

I think of sending her back to the village. But then I know that even if I get another one, Ishaka will seduce her as well. He is now beyond repair and seems to get attracted to these girls the way a cat reacts to milk. My dear Ishaka simply can't let an H.G. be; not when she is under his roof and he is paying her salary. You'd get a better deal asking the *malwa* fly to spend a night under the same roof with a pot of freshly brewed *malwa* and leave it untouched. Or asking Bwana Fisi, the Hyena, to roast some succulent beef and expect him not to taste any of it. Isn't it this same hyena who, in a rare moment of honesty, once advised those who had come to bury his mother-in-law to 'bury her very far because hearts are not the same?'

So I let her – the housegirl – be after a serious warning. Yes, now she is a housegirl, not H.G.

But it doesn't take long before *something* happens.

Ishaka comes home one night; no, one morning, from the *Mzungu* point of view. I clearly hear the car entering the garage – the sound is unmistakable. I also clearly hear him opening the back door and locking it. I wait for him to come to the bedroom in vain. Where the hell can he be? This particular night I am not just some loyal wife waiting for the so-called breadwinner to be back home. No way. I am also one hungry weasel waiting to be attended to. There are stirrings deep within me that need some male attention to be put to rest. I am one garden hungry for the farmer's hoe in due season. Yes, I want Ishaka this time; it has been so long since he last had his way with me. Just this once will do no harm, after which each will roll to their side of the bed. In road distances that is something like one being in Kampala city and the other in Kasese town; over 300 km apart.

So where the hell is Ishaka?

Maybe there is a burglar who has been lying in wait for him; lurking in one of the dark corners and waiting to clobber him as soon as he comes in.

The thought sends a cold chill down my spine. Even though I have this love-hate thing towards Ishaka because of the way he has injured me, still I don't want him dead. For damn it, I bear his name and he is the father of my children.

There are certain men and women who say that they would rather lose the one they love than share him or her. I do not fall in that category.

I stealthily get out of bed, careful not to make a single creak. I must go on this rescue mission.

I grope under the bed and get out the stick I use for pounding millet. I know this sounds rural but actually I do pound my own millet. There are certain foods I can never buy from the market and millet flour is one of them.

I arm myself with this weapon. The pounding stick, I mean. I am not like some women who will pick a slipper with which to attack the formidable enemy. This is by no chance intended to belittle the sisterhood fraternity. But I have *ink* (indisputable evidence) that in more homes than I care to mention, when heavily armed thugs strike, the man of the house gets a *panga* or some such keen instrument to attack while the woman gets her worn out *slipper* with which to attack!

Well, for crying out loud!

Holding my breath, I walk slowly, quietly like the padded cat. I suddenly feel brave enough to rescue my husband. Not that I am brave all the time. It is just that when fear is countered by even a bigger fear, bravery is the result. In this case, my fear of the unknown future without Ishaka is a million times greater than the fear of darkness or robbers.

Where the hell can the thief be? And if he has already injured my husband, where could he have dumped him?

Stop! There is a noise from one of the children's bedrooms. Do I hear somebody being strangled? Oh my poor husband! That must be him, clearly breathing his last, gasping for breath. I have never heard him in such agony, the poor man. Between the gasps, he cries out for his mother, poor thing.

'Oh, you are killing me!' He groans. The last words of a dying man, I am sure.

With all the force I can muster, I kick open the bedroom door and switch on the light. I raise the pounding stick high, ready to finish off the murderer as in the same breath I let off this ear-piercing screech followed by the most urgent sounding, fear-filled alarm of all time.

'*Walalala, walalala*! Help! Thieves! My husband is being murdered! Heeeeeeelp!'

The neighbourhood hears the alarm. It was enough to wake the dead; much more than enough to call heaven to attention and even bring all creation to a standstill.

They pick it up and within a minute, Village Eleven – the name of this haven of ours is resounding with different degrees of alarm. It is amazing what one woman's cry can do to an entire neighbourhood. We may pretend to be ladies who can't speak beyond a whisper just because we are around men, or to be precise, when they are all around us. But when faced with the possibility of disaster our true selves come out and they are seldom as pretty as our faces.

Some of the rescue team have whistles, which they used in the last Presidential campaign and they blow them until their lungs almost burst. Others get their drums and bang away on them without any particular sense of rhythm (you can't blame them; this is no time for celebration). Yet others get tins of one type or another and clang them with such fury and urgency, this time the din is enough to send a pregnant elephant straight into the labour ward, with immediate results. Solidarity. If there is an attribute our people have in abundance, this is it: solidarity.

It is called *munno mukabi* in local speak. Something like when your neighbour is in danger, it becomes your business. Great idea.

In the rural areas, they have these associations called *twezikye* – let's bury one another. Still on the same line as *munno mukabi.*

So when somebody dies, it is the obligation of everyone around to contribute either money, food or firewood. There is a book where everything is recorded. You fail to go for the burial, you are noted down. You will suffer alone when you lose a loved one. Or if you do not take any contribution for the burial, when you lose somebody, you will be paid in your own coins. I don't mind all these schemes. But what bothers me is why these people never think of forming associations for *cure*. Like setting up a fund where everybody contributes so that should a member fall sick and does not have the money for treatment, there will be that money in the fund to take care of the patient. So instead of the *Twezikye* associations only, there will be the *Twetambire* (let's cure ourselves) ones as well.

But sometimes I think our people think real queer. When there is death they will come wailing and will gladly offer huge amounts of money in commiseration. But then they will not willingly come to the rescue of a patient who is in need of treatment but has no money.

My household is awake now and they all appear with different types of weapons, all assorted and ferocious-looking enough to scare the wits out of any of Napoleon's generals.

The H.B. looks mighty fierce with the iron and the *shamba* boy is the picture of a World War II veteran with his slasher. I am really lucky that these people have hearkened to my cry for help. Under normal circumstances or is it abnormal (when Ishaka is attempting to whip me silly), they would have covered their heads with their blankets not wanting to be involved in the dangerous situation. Never involve yourself in a fight between lovers. They will team up against you instead and all your rescue intentions will earn you a thrashing you could have done without.

All this I notice within the twinkling of an eye.

'I will kill you, thief!' I scream as I raise the pounding stick to strike.

'Where is he so that we finish him off?' The rest of the *army* shout in unison. Quite some unity around here, I tell you!

Then suddenly, I start screaming.

'Madam, have you found the master's body?' The *shamba* boy asks as one of the neighbours breaks out in mourning. She is joined by some other neighbour and between them, they raise up this ear splitting din.

That neighbour, she is some sort of professional mourner for Chrissake! Don't you be taken in by her dry-eyed act. There is this one time when she is passing near some church, on a weekday. A service is going on, and seeing the many cars parked outside, she assumes somebody must be dead.

Immediately, she starts crying as she enters the church and finds a seat.

'Oh the poor handsome, the *late*! To die at such a tender age!'

Heads turn to look at her strangely.

'Madam', the person next to her says in a dry voice. 'This is a *thanksgiving* service.'

But I should not dismiss her just as a professional mourner. She may be feeling *genuinely* sad. There are people who are touched by the death of *anybody* – relative or not.

Back to the horror scene involving my husband.

I keep on screaming. God, I can't believe my eyes. My husband was groaning in pain, my foot! The bastard was groaning in *ecstasy*! For here he is on top of the housegirl! And he is not on top of her to perform some urgent humanitarian act like artificial respiration. Not exactly, by any means. And the housegirl is most certainly not having any problem with this arrangement. No attempt to throw him off, at least none that I can see.

I just start throwing up, most of it landing on the writhing shameless couple. They look decidedly evil. I swear they do. I am looking at two reptiles *coiled* all over each other and certainly not complaining about lack of space or anything like that. They have hectares of space all round: this room can actually host a public rally with ease.

'Get out! Get out!' I order the war veterans. God! They should not have witnessed such an embarrassing tragedy.

Meanwhile the occupants of Village Eleven have all streamed into the house. They are in no doubt that Ishaka has been murdered.

'Oh poor Ishaka. To die like a thief!' One of them wails.

'Shut up. He is not dead.' Not yet anyway, I add under my breath.

I shoo them out of the room telling them that thanks to their cooperation, the thieves have run away. Oh, you are such nice neighbours. Nice having you around, good night and God bless you all, let's talk some more tomorrow.

Meantime, the two *lust* birds are trying to cover their nakedness. When I see the lecherous housegirl trying to cover her field of battle with her hand, I pass out and when I come to, I find my so-called husband fanning me. At the sight of him I mercifully pass out again. I say mercifully, because I can't stand the sight of him.

I spend the rest of the night in some kind of semi-conscious state. It is as if I am on the crest of a huge wave. It *sucks* me in and brings me up again. Up and down. I am riding on the crest of this huge wave. Then I go down, under it, and get up with a gasp of breathlessness. I open my eyes wide only to be met with the looming face of a *seemingly* concerned Ishaka fanning my face.

'My dear, welcome back from the land of semi-consciousness. Please relax and take things easy,' he croons.

'How?' I ask inwardly. Take things easy, my nail! How *unfeeling* can people get? *Some* things you *may* take easy. But when you find a thief *eating* your well-kept food, how *easy* can you take it? Especially when the menu is supposed to be strictly *personal* to the holder?

Actually, the bastard sounds genuinely concerned but it must be because he thinks I might die *on him*. From the shock of catching him and that louse of a girl at the frontline. So he is worried about himself not about *me*. Like in the event that something dreadful did happen to me, what would he tell the children and my clan? Especially since he knows that everybody knew how his womanising was practically sending me over the bend.

Sometimes a woman will mourn because her husband has betrayed his marriage vows to her by turning left or right. But it is also true that quite often a woman will weep not because of the husband's unfaithfulness (it is only a handful of naïve women that ever expect a man to be faithful), but because of his complete disregard and lack of taste. In my case, it is both. How can I share a man with my own housegirl?

'Please my dear darling, relax.'

I want to ask him how in the name of my cows I can relax but I am too weak to bring out anything intelligible. All I manage is a feeble spit right in his damn eye before I drift into another restless kind of sleep – if I can call it that.

Then I have this dream. I am a mermaid and seated on a rock in the middle of the sea. I am enjoying the lovely sunshine as I watch the fish dive in and out of the deep blue water. I am so happy that I decide to ride on the crest of a wave. It is here that I feel closest to my creator. It is also here that I think with fondest memories about Ishaka. Then my friend Fina calls out to me from the shore:

'Liz, don't marry that man Ishaka.'

'And why shouldn't I marry him? I love him and he loves me too.'

'But you are a mermaid and he is a human being. You cannot find happiness together.'

The sound of the waves grows louder in my ears. A mist covers the shore. Then from the mist, a figure emerges. It is Ishaka. Tall, elegant and handsome. He is a *he* man, not a *beautiful* male. I don't like beautiful men. He is so handsome I catch my breath at his breathtaking looks.

Slowly, he moves towards me. He stretches out his hand to me. I hold my hand out and put it in his. He pulls me to his chest and into his chest and our lips merge in an endless kiss that defines a lovely moment that will forever be etched in my memory.

I momentarily wake up and wonder why I am having this dream. Then I remember that I have just been reading this book *The Little Mermaid* by somebody or other.

There was this Prince who lived near the sea and liked to swim. For the first few months he went there simply to swim. But soon he admitted to himself that there was a more pressing and compelling reason for the frequent visits to the sea.

A beautiful mermaid in that sea – aren't they all cute anyway? – always sat on a rock in the middle of the day to enjoy the sun. Soon keen observers noticed that whenever the Prince swam, the mermaid was perched on the rock enjoying the sunshine. But some said it was the other way round; that the truth of the matter was that whenever the mermaid was perched on the rock, the Prince was sure to be found swimming.

Eventually they fall in love with each other. Or rather admit, each to the other, that they are in love, since for all intents and purposes each had fallen for the other but was either too shy or too proud to confess.

The Prince proposes, only to find out that his diction is entirely superfluous – the Mermaid is already abuzz about him and makes it clear that she had in fact already said 'yes', only that he had not yet asked.

The Mermaid was evidently a sincere believer in the Ruth of the Bible who left her land of Moab to go to Israel, telling Naomi 'Your people will be my people and your God my God.'

She left the sea and walked or rather *hobbled* – she was moving upright on her tail with the greatest difficulty – home with the man of her heart.

But it was not the easiest of walks or hobbles. Evidently God had not had it in plan for half-fish-half-human creatures to consort with full-blown humans and as such had not put in place any contingency provision for walking should some of them be so crazy as to indulge in the incredible.

The tail had plenty of scales, fine; but they proved no protection against the tough gravel that the road was made of and did not afford her any comfort. So she suffered double – the discomfort of walking instead of swimming and the excruciating pain as the stones and gravel tore into her tail, bloodying her all over.

But this was no time for tears – it would not do to cry even before the marriage had been consummated. The young man would probably change his mind. Not an enthusing prospect when she considered that the land had only one Prince and more importantly, she was madly in love with him.

In her love she was blind yes, but not too blind to realise that she would not last too long in the land of the humans if walking was to be part of her daily routine. She quickly ruled out any possibility of romantic walks, however inviting the moonlight proved.

Something told her things could be easier if her man would carry her. But obviously the Prince did not care for such small time romantics and in any case, a nice look-over told her the young man's muscle would not shoulder such a burden. The upper part of her body was okay; but her fish tail was humongous – probably 100kg, the kind of weight even the strongest man could only manage once in a long while.

After a few days, the Mermaid's fears proved a huge under-estimate. Though there was no problem in the bedroom – the royal nest was certainly well feathered and His Highness' performance in bed was not bad at all; in fact it was much better than the quick-as-a-winkle fish variety she was used to witnessing – the rest was disaster.

First, it was hard to get around. Walking was too painful. Each step she took even to the washroom was like a thousand knives cutting into her.

Soon she decided that *Bwana Bata* the duck who had exchanged feet with *Bwana Jogoo,* the cock and failed to float on the water (while Jogoo hen couldn't even scratch for worms in the yard) had fared much better than she.

Yes, she and the Prince were in love, but love alone would not be enough to sustain this marriage. It would take more than just love to sustain a union of two radically different elements.

She did not wait for a royal send-off as she was sure there would not be one and certainly not a pleasant one if ever there was any. She hobbled painfully back to her element and weeping, threw herself on the crest of a wave and became foam.

I slip back into the restless sleep. I dream about the agonised face of the mermaid. Above the haze of the waves, the silhouette of her sad face emerges. She gives me this sad smile and whispers:

'Don't cry for me, Liz. I did not keep my Prince but at least I am back in my element.'

I momentarily come back to my present circumstances.

"Are you in your element?" I ask of this figure looming above me.

"What *element* dear?" The horror lurking above me is asking. Oh, it is *him*!

But what is Ishaka's element? Some people have no element; they have never found themselves. They are just adrift; trying to find the missing link and looking for it in dip tanks that can never hold anything. They are hollow. Trying to find fulfilment in one person and when they fail, move on to the next, never settling. Just like a bird always on the wing or that notorious weed, the Wandering Jew, showing up everywhere without being anywhere.

'Just leave me alone,' I say wearily, too weak to fight verbally.

'The Little Mermaid.' I dig that story. I really do. The message is great. I mean about remaining in one's element and that sort of thing.

People like Ishaka have not found themselves, so they look for meaning not only in the flesh but also in the supernatural. I have indisputable evidence that Ishaka goes to look for his lost self at a place called *Ibaare rya Mugore* (rock of the bride); a place whose legend has been told and retold to me by my good old grandma :

During the reign of the Chwezi dynasty in western Uganda, there was a Mchwezi called Mugasha whose residence was on a hill called Mugore in Nyabushozi County.

Mugasha's favourite pastime was curing tobacco and telling people to keep away from his well – a very deep one – from which he bathed.

'Never pass too close to my well', he always said. But either they were hard of hearing or simply possessed the obstinacy that a donkey would envy. Somehow, few people paid attention.

One day as he was bathing, a bridal entourage came by. They were on their way from *okuhingira* (marriage ceremony) in Kabagore.

In those days a bride was carried in a hammock with a huge umbrella *(enkinga)* hanging overhead, shielding her from whatever sunshine, rain or queer aspect of the weather threatened to spoil her beauty. This was no time for someone to look less than perfect.

Presently, as the sun went through his wind-up formalities for the day, sinking slowly in the distance and just for good measure sending out a warm glow, making a great and glorious sunset, the bridal entourage came by Mugasha bathing at the wellside.

The sight of a naked man, body glistening in the sunset and manhood dangling like a cucumber was the perfect recipe for mirth.

The party was already in a festive mood after a successful marriage ceremony and decided this comical dimension was simply the perfect icing on the cake; the superlative way to end a great day.

No reason why one should not have a good laugh – never mind it was at the expense of a fellow feeling most embarrassed. Laugh they did, loud and long.

It turned out to be the biggest error they ever made in their lifetime. It was also the last thing they ever did on the planet earth.

The Chwezi were gods, or so they were believed to be. More importantly they believed themselves to be. The idea of mortal beings violating the never-pass-by-here law laid down by the gods was bad enough. Seeing a god stark naked was worse. But then laughing at him was the ultimate. From the god's point of view, the bridal party had simply compounded their errors by committing the unforgivable sin. They had poked their fingers into the eyes of a god and then rubbed salt and pepper therein.

An emotion cocktail shot through the god's mind – anger, irritation, bitterness and the determination to revenge. No one could see the immortals naked and live to tell the story.

Without bothering to cover himself – they had seen everything anyway – he raised his voice and cursed them bitterly, *ni mukacwekye amamunengye.*

The entire bridal entourage turned into stones. The god scooped some more water, poured it casually over his body and the bath continued as though nothing had happened.

To this day the place is called *Ibaare rya mugore* (rock of the bride). The rock still retains some distinct features that bear testimony to the legend.

A keen observer will notice that one of the stones is shaped precisely like a bride, head covered with a veil that protrudes beyond the forehead. It is surrounded by smaller stones that were her entourage, frozen for time and eternity by the words that came from the mouth of a god.

Nearby is a huge rock with a huge cave where Mugasha used to hold court. Inside the cave are small stones, stools on which the people sat as Mugasha passed judgement on his mortal subjects. A short distance away is the well where Mugasha used to bathe, called Kyamugama. It is believed to be one of the deepest wells in the world.

The Chwezi dynasty remains enshrouded in mysticism and mystery. But it nevertheless holds a special place in many hearts.

The stones are testimony that people's belief that the Chwezi were more god than human was no idle persuasion. Even today, in modern Uganda, many people in western Uganda still believe in the deity of the Chwezi. Many still go to worship the Chwezi gods and often call upon them in the day of trouble, in the time of need.

The first Chwezi is believed to have been Isimbwa, son of Ishaza, the Omukama (King) of Kitara. Isimbwa's mother, they say, was Nyamate, daughter of Ruyonga, Omugabe (King) of Ankole. Ndahura, one of Isimbwa's descendants was the father of Mugasha.

At the Rocks of Mugore is a small shrine where people bow, then kneel on the ground beside the rock and then pray for anything. It is widely believed that people's wishes are granted.

* * *

One day I decide to go and look at this place where I know Ishaka goes. We drive up to St. Gonzaga Mugore Primary School, that lies just below the rocks. I ask a youth if I could get a guide to take me up to the rocks.

Soon a middle-aged woman called Dorotiya comes along and I learn she is my guide.

Dorotiya first wants to know our respective clans. She clarifies that if one belongs to the Basingo clan, the place is out of bounds.

The Basingo are believed to be the people who brought permanent death. It was believed that people always resurrected some day. One day when a Musingo noticed somebody rising from their grave he attacked saying, 'go back, the dead should never resurrect'. The corpse went back to its grave and since then, folklore goes, people have never resurrected again.

Since I am not a Musingo, up we go.

Not exactly romantic, this place.

The way up is not too steep, but enough to make you pant if you are physically unfit. There is no path, you simply trudge through bush.

As we get nearer I feel some unease, some eerie feeling, as though there is some whispering wind all round. Matters are not helped by a drizzle that has created a misty atmosphere around the rocks. Clearly this is no place for the faint-hearted.

But I shake my head and tell myself 'Come on now, you are an educated woman; you ought to be more composed.'

'Isn't there some elderly person who looks after this place?' I ask Dorotiya. She answers that the old woman who used to look after the place died a few years ago. The day she was buried people saw things, Dorotiya assures me.

'People saw lanterns in the air,' Dorotiya explains. When I probe her further she gets furious. "I say they saw many things, don't ask too many questions. That is the problem with you educated people.

Why don't you just take things as you are told?"

Later I ask a group of villagers who have gathered at the foot of the hill, whether it wouldn't be a good idea if they could clear the tall grass and shrubs so that there is a clear path to the rocks.

I discuss with them the possibility of building huts, a small kind of resort where people can come and rest, tour the place and appreciate the way of life of the local people.

I tell them that what they have on them is a fantastic tourist attraction, which the whole world ought to come and know about. I explain something about community-based tourism to them.

Dorotiya says it's okay to build huts far below the rocks, but not near them.

'An unseen fire will come and burn them,' she explains. 'This place is sacred; it is the sanctuary of the gods.'

As we drive back to Kampala, I ponder these issues. Then all of a sudden the driver stops the car abruptly.

'What's the matter?' I ask.

As he jumps out of the car he is excitedly shouting 'Money, money!'

'What money?' I ask him.

'There is money in the road,' he exclaims, pointing.

I get out of the car and, true to fact, there is money lying right in the middle of the road.

The young man is quickly on his knees, picking up the money – in denominations of 1000 – as though he is picking *ensenene* (grasshoppers). You'd think a box dropped off a bullion van. We count shillings 125,000.

I ask him to put the money together so we can take it to the area Local Council (LC) Chairman, as it seems it has fallen from somebody's pocket.

The driver says I must be joking. 'This is my money,' he says. 'I prayed at the shrine of Mugore and told the gods I badly needed some money. How do you know the LC Chairman won't take the money himself, anyway?'

But I insist and we give the money to the LC Chairman.

Luckily enough, I have shillings 125,000 on me, which I give to my driver.

He smiles. 'There! The gods have truly answered my prayer.'

I try for hours on end to convince him that this was mere coincidence, but at the end of the day it turns out I have nicely wasted my time and breath.

* * *

By the time I pull myself together and try to get over the disastrous incident of Ishaka on top of the housegirl (yes, she is a housegirl now not the H. G.) it is approaching nine in the morning. Sunday morning. I must pull myself together and go to church. I have to wear this cheerful attitude, yet within, I am going through hell. I get ready for church and head for the nine o'clock service.

The hymns the Reverend has selected do not disappoint me. It is as though he knows what I have just gone through. I put all my heart into the singing. I feel uplifted and I actually feel as if heavy stuff is falling off from within and without my body. Tears of cleansing course down my cheeks and as I weep, I at the same time smile through the tears.

Time now to go to the Holy Table. I kneel down and extend my hand for the bread. Then a familiar male perfume wafts to my nostrils. I recognise it: it is only one man in the world who wears it. I know it because it is me who has the formula: I mix four different perfumes to get it.

The beast!

'You,' I hiss at him. 'What the hell do you think *you* are doing here?'

'Same as you. I have come for holy communion.'

'Holy what? You just make me sick. You dare come to kneel before God when this morning I caught you with your *tail* between the house-girl's legs?'

The vision of his glistening member, looking like a snake, as it emerged out of the housegirl's you-know-what floats across my eyes. Only that this time I am seeing a real snake, disturbed in its regular deep afternoon slumber and looking around in surprise, head turning this way and that way as it tries to internalise what is happening all round, before coiling in resignation and dropping off to sleep.

I am so pissed off I hadn't realised that I am shouting. All around me are in shock at this couple, looking like two exasperated raccoons preparing to attack each other.

'Please Madam, you are before the Holy Table!'

'With such scum trying to make a mockery of God's wonderful gift to mankind?' I shoot back as I contemptuously curve my thumb towards Ishaka.

I give the bread back to the priest and storm out with the grace of a soccer hooligan mad at the referee who has refused to award his team a redeeming penalty in injury time.

'Liz, remember Jesus came to save sinners like me,' Ishaka shouts after me.

Anyway, If I ever see that toad again at the Holy Table, it's quits for me. I mean, it loses sense when a man was caught *at it* and his member seen withdrawing from the well of iniquity. Glittering with the fluid of sin and all. (Puke, puke.) And then the following day, he comes to the Holy Table looking holier than the Angel Gabriel. You should see him with that pious look that sent my stomach into real olympics. Arms folded across his chest. Looking so angelic you can think any time you will see this glowing halo around his head. I mean!

The cat with cream all over his lips is pleading not guilty to charges of breaking into the dairy next door.

There is this sick feeling in the pit of my stomach. And this is the kind of fellow who comes to kneel next to, not holy people as such, but human beings who try to be decent although they do get occasional lapses. Sinners yes, but who try not to consciously hurt their partners. I mean, to screw the housegirl in my house! At least if he had taken her to some bloody lodge or wherever else. This man Ishaka has the manners of a cat and the morals of a weasel.

* * *

So as I was saying up there, even if I sacked this girl and brought in a new one, it would be the same story. Ishaka would pounce on her. It is not wisdom throwing out the frog and bringing in the lizard.

His philosophy is: it does not matter whether he has sex with a graduate or an illiterate village calico because after all, he asks, does a vagina go to school? What obscene rubbish!

And therein lies the fundamental difference between men's and women's sexuality: most men have sex with only the vagina while women have sex with the whole man and not just his penis.

* * *

Some of these modern girls are very daring. And I say bravo to them because they teach the philandering men a thing or two about how *not* to handle a woman. None of their usual pick, play and drop formula; using a girl for two or three days then discarding her like a used condom without a further thought.

Like this other girl who comes to see me one hot afternoon.

I am lounging on the sofa when I hear this knock on the door. When I open, I am greeted by the warm smile of this twenty-something girl. She is holding this huge Bible.

'Come in my dear," I invite her. "Have we met before?'

'Yes, Madam. We go to the same church. I always see you on Sundays. Then there is this friend of yours whom I asked to direct me here and she kindly did.'

'Have a seat. What do you do?'

'I am a pastor," she says.

'Oh how wonderful! At such a young age too!'

'I know. Everybody marvels at it. God called me at a tender age. He gave me special powers and whatever I pray for comes to pass.'

I get up and hug her. I am sure God has specifically sent her to me.

'Incidentally, what's your name?'

'Pastor Moreen.'

'My dear Pastor, you have come at the right time. There is this emptiness within me, a void...' My voice trails off. I feel tears stinging my eyes.

The Pastor takes me in her young arms and gives me a take-courage hug.

'You see, Madam, you must take away the pain before you can begin to live again,' she says softly.

Such wonderful words from one so young!

'Let's pray,' and we kneel down humble and all.

'Father, you are the one who knows the wounds in our hearts, you are the one who can give us the injection that will put us together again. Give us the drip of life, Father. Amen.'

'Amen,' I echo.

Then she opens the Bible and begins to read: 'Hear these words of comfort: 'Come unto me all that labour and are heavy laden and I will give you rest.' Then she pauses. 'Madam, do you have faith that what we are going to pray for will come to pass?'

'Oh yes. I do. I do.' Although sometimes I am not sure I do. Who is it that said belief is knowing that it is going to rain and faith is carrying an umbrella?

'Then, Madam, come and kneel down here before the Lord and we pray for deliverance.' Which I hasten to do. She places her hands on my head but before she can break out in prayer, Ishaka enters. His mouth flies open and the briefcase drops from his hands.

'My God!' He exclaims in an almost inaudible voice. 'What the hell is going on here?' He asks incredulously.

'Shhh,' I whisper with my finger on my lips. 'Ishaka, you are interrupting an important session.'

'What *session*?' He asks incredulously.

'This young lady is touched with the power of God. She is a Pastor and God has led her here to share His word with me.'

'Pastor? What Pastor?' He asks in shock.

'She is Pastor Moreen. Has been a Pastor since the tender age of fifteen. Got a special calling.'

Ishaka roars into this dry laughter.

'If she is a Pastor, then I am the Pope and my father is alive,' he declares. His father died 10 years ago. Then with grim determination, he hauls the pastor to her feet.

'And you vixen, just get out of my house before I whistle for the dogs to do it.'

'Give me my money and I go, or else I will tell your wife all about it.' Meanwhile, she is looking daggers at him. 'I warned you that I would do something you wouldn't like, didn't I?'

'What's going on here?' I am smelling foul play.

'It's this man. He is a liar. He promised to marry ...'

Ishaka pushes her out as she yells obscenities at him. He refuses to tell me what had happened. But I am not a fool. He obviously had moments of lust with her, which she construed to mean that he was in love with her. Then he backed off and she started tracking him and eventually hatches up this plan of coming to his home and embarrassing him in front of his wife thereby hoping to ruin his marriage irreversibly.

Pastor Moreen! She certainly had me hooked to her mad scheme. I must give her credit for her ingenuity, apart from being a first class actress.

She is such a gifted liar, I wager she should consider running for political office!

* * *

Oh I wish I could sleep for even ten minutes! But the damn sleep is refusing to come.

Then I recall the advice Fina gave me in case sleeplessness shows up at a time when every soul ought to be in slumberland.

That I should imagine a situation where there are fifty sheep trying to jump over a fence. Then I should start counting each sheep as it runs towards the fence and jumps over it.

Great. No harm in trying every remedy. Even a stupid-sounding one like this one. Desperate situations need desperate remedies, so they say.

Let me start.

Sheep number one: a very fat one. It is so fat I can hardly see its eyes which are hidden by a layer of fat. It is *neckless.* What passes as its neck are folds after folds of fat. It has got a huge wobbly stomach.

By my estimation this one would not show up for the census of virgins. Most likely place to hang out: the antenatal clinic. Favourite pastime: cuddling and kissing. And maybe, she won't admit it, sex. How many lovers has she had? How many men (in the sheep sense) have seen her nakedness? More than one? Did she settle with the man who first kissed her, the one who first took her panties off, the one who first unwrapped her from her diapers? Well, what business of mine is it?

So sheep number one, mama-to-be, let me flag you off. On your marks, get set, go!

I lie back and watch sheep number one as it wobbles along towards the fence. Eh! Careful now!

There is a log across the path. Or what the Good Book calls a stumbling stone, a rock of offence. Something put there for the sole purpose of making your life difficult. Oh you didn't see it in time and you have tripped over it, poor sheep.

Come on get up. We always fall down in life but we have to make an effort and rise up again. That is what we mean by overcoming the world. Certainly that is what the Lord had in mind when he told Adam to subdue the earth and rule over it. That means nothing ever comes easy, we have always got to take command of every situation and determine never to be put down for ever. The important thing is not that you fell, rather whether, after falling, you stayed down and moaned like a pregnant cow having a pity party, or you got up, dusted yourself, held your head high and marched on.

There you are, good girl. Up you get. Wasn't easy was it? Once you are down, getting up is not all that easy especially if all sorts of weights are bearing you down.

Funny how we women can be; we never enjoy having somebody subdue us and weigh us down. But when it comes to sex we make an exception to the rule. We will gladly be weighed down and held down for hours on end, without complaining a single bit. Then when the man changes his mind and wants to release us, we exclaim in exasperation and ask what is wrong.

Run, girl, run. The fence is not too far off now. However, remember the old dictum: that when you are carrying a load on your head, the nearer you get to your destination, the heavier the load grows. Talking of loads again; isn't it funny that the heaviest men, bellies protruding like the bass drum of a marching band, have the tiniest women in their beds. Never you despise a woman because she is tiny; the loads they carry are incredible. And believe you me, that is one of the only few occasions when a woman will not subscribe to this Biblical injunction to help carry one another's burdens. She will be only too happy to carry that particular burden all alone, thank you very much. If anything, should fate tempt you to help her, she will most kindly improve your appearance with a bowl of concentrated sulphuric or hydrochloric acid. Funny how quick and adept with acid incensed women lovers can be, even when they failed chemistry at school. Even if they had no end of trouble comprehending the numerous theories and formulae in chemistry class and in fact had to be recalled for further instruction in that same class on more than one occasion, women somehow make no mistakes with acid.

Ah, you are now gathering momentum to jump over the fence. Up and over to the other side. Fine. Let me give you a well-deserved clap. Clap, clap.

Now then, sheep number two: Get ready. The whistle is blowing. You are not as fat as number one. No, no. Let me make you fatter than number one. Then it means you will take a longer time than number one to reach the damn fence. If she was three months pregnant, I will make you five and a half months pregnant. Any time from now you will be gracing the labour ward and sending forth two or three lambs. If you were unfaithful to your regular husband, you could be in trouble. If he is brown, your litter had better be the same. Or else you will be like the woman who, like her husband, was as dark as charcoal but who brought forth a kid whiter than a European. Apparently the woman, a sincere advocate of the adage that the first cut is the deepest, spent a busy hour (during her honeymoon in London) in some hotel with the white man who pierced her maidenhead when she was still in high school.

Her poor husband doted over her pregnancy like a spoiled kid, only for him to be deflated painfully when he took a good long look at what he had until then regarded as his first child.

That only served to reinforce my belief that many a man who marries a non-virgin may occasionally be at the mercy of whoever had the privilege of taking away his wife's innocence, especially if the said man proves to be a moron..

One, two, go! Trot, and there you jump.

I begin yawning as I call upon sheep number three. By the time I reach number eleven, I am so bored that I threaten to forget about the whole project. Project send Liz to sleep. The proposal was written by Fina, if you please.

Sheep number th—thirrrr—thirteeeeeeeeeeeeee—nnnnnnnn. This yawning is too much. The whole bloody exercise is too boring. Now I can hardly even see the damn sheep! There is this dirty white one which is wobbling before my eyes. But why do I have to count the sheep, anyway? I might as well imagine Malai jumping over the fence because there is absolutely no difference between her and those sheep, except that her legs are like toothpicks while those of the sheep are short and fat. Both physically and mentally.

So get ready, Malai. Go jump over the fence. On your marks, get set, go! Ha, ha haaaaaaaaaaa! Look how she is hobbling on her needle-thin legs!

Oh sweet sleep. You are verrrrry, veeeeeee—rrrrrrrrry welcome. You aaaree—yaaaawwwwwnnnnnnnn—such a rare visitor ttt—to me these dddddddd-d-days. In any cccccc-case, you are the only visitor who can be welcomed to anybody's home at this ungodly hour of the night. Sorry, morning in Muzungu speak. Ummmmmm. *Karibu ssana mama* sl-sleee… All of a sudden, I am wide awake. I realise that I have referred to sleep as *mama*!

Yes, she must be a woman, a *mother*. Sleep I mean. Caring, warm. Wanting you her child to take a rest from life's troubled. Which are like housework. For you can never finish housework. You finish cleaning here only to see dirt in the other corner. You jump there and when you finish it you think all is fine. Only to realise a cobweb hanging on the ceiling bulb and so on and so forth and all that sort of thing. And so *ad infinitum*. Jumping from one place to another, restlessly like a grasshopper. We have been reduced to winged insects.

The minute I think of sleep as a mother, *my* mom, I feel this calmness settle over me. I see her open her arms wide and I enter her warm embrace. I am surrounded by motherly love and I am transported so many years back.

I am a child and mother is giving me milk. I take it as I look into her eyes. Mom, I never got time to tell you how much I loved you, how *all* the family loved you.

'Shhh. I know you did love me, you still love me all of you my children. Although I left you many years ago, physically. Think of me as just being in another country. Shhh, my child. Go to sleep now. I have brought you a lovely dream, my dear.'

And as she lovingly passes her finger over my eyebrows over and over, she softly sings that lullaby I used to love so much:

Dreams to sell **fine** dreams to sell,
Angus is here with dreams to sell,

Hush you my baby and sleep **without** fear....

Dream Angus has brought you a dream my dear....

Mmmmmmmmmmmm...

My eyelids grow heavy. I try to keep her face in focus but it is getting blurred.

Mom, I will never suffer from sleeplessness again. I have now discovered the medicine to my insomnia – you Mom.

Imagine, Mom, it took me so many years to get the solution to my sleeplessness: just the memory of you holding me close to your breast as you used to do when I was a child...Don't think I am forgetting how good you too were, Papa... yours was masculine comfort; the type that will give you a firm foundation to chart your way in life ...very important, Papa, that one...but it will not make you think of gentle hands rocking you to sleep...but, Papa, the combination of rock strength and gentle breeze is crucial... oh sweeeeeet sleeeeeep...

CHAPTER TWO

RUDE AWAKENING

'Good-morning dear. You have overslept today. Have you forgotten that we are going to Kololo airstrip for the Independence Anniversary celebrations?'

Who is this impertinent human interrupting my hard-earned sleep? Sleep does not come easy, especially if you are feeling out of favour with the Almighty.

Counting those lousy sheep was nothing to write home about, my friend. When you start counting sheep, the next embarkation will, without doubt, be to the mental asylum!

And the way I am carrying on, I am nearing that dreaded place; to join that little world whose inhabitants think the rest of the world does not understand. I hear mad people think and understand; but only in a certain way that is different from the rest of us. And from *their* point of view yes, they do have points of view – the rest of us are mad and we just don't know how things should be done.

After all, in the Bible aren't we told how King Nebuchadnezzar – stupid man – thought he could cheat God of the glory? The Almighty sentenced him to seven years madness, until he would be able to understand and appreciate that promotion and power come from God not from anywhere else and that He gives it to whomsoever He wills. How could Nebuchadnezzar, a madman, understand, if mad people have no minds? So I can safely say Nebuchadnezzar was fully conscious of what was happening, except for a few things.

First, for growing airs that offended the Almighty he was punished by growing hairs of a beast. He saw nothing wrong with eating grass and found he was able to chew the cud very naturally. He drank water direct from the wells and streams, saw no use for clothing and strutted about very comfortably in Adam's suit. He did his toilet in the middle of the street as everybody looked on in disgust, mated with other animals in the open, enjoying every moment of it – as some other men enjoyed his wives and concubines.

Of course the wives had to find someone to do the needful. There is no such thing as a fallow period when it comes to times like these. If the man is mad and is making love to the sheep in the pasture and the cows by the brook, why not get you some good solid son of something to satiate your desires? No point in letting your mortar grow weeds when there are pestles all around to keep thc weeds out.

Really I think no one is really mad at all; mad folks are simply people with different points of view.

Talking of which I think I have, like King Nebuchadnezzar, developed a different point of view. Take the nights. I go check whether the taps are closed more than ten times each night!

As I am about to fall asleep, I get a panic attack. Oh, my God! I must have left the kitchen tap half closed. And I must have left on the stopper. The sink will overflow and the house will flood. Then the entire family will drown. May God be with us.

I quickly jump out of bed and dash to the kitchen expecting the house to have flooded already.

I make straight to the tap. No water is dripping from it. I give a huge sigh of relief.

As I trace my way back to the bedroom, I get another panic attack. Maybe *this* time I really did not close the tap tightly enough.

I dash back to the kitchen. In my panicky hurry, I tumble over the dining table, which comes on top of me. Help! This table is raping me, I scream. Damn! My nightdress has gotten torn in the process – am looking every inch a rape victim.

I retrieve what is left of the nightie and continue on my mission.

I reach the kitchen, my heart in my mouth. Straight to the tap. Whew! My relief-filled breath whistles out. No dripping water, tap tightly closed. But just to be 100% sure, I re-tighten the damn tap.

I am not very convinced though that it is completely closed tight. Then I devise a way which will not leave me doubting as to whether or not I have done it properly – by introducing a religious angle to it. I decide that I will tighten the tap seven times as I mentally say, 'Jesus, Jesus.' Gotcha.

I proceed to do exactly that.

Satisfied, I begin the journey back to the bedroom. Oh God! Maybe in my over-zealousness to tighten the tap, I instead reopened it and the water would flow and the house would flood...

As I make a U–turn to go back to the kitchen, I smell something burning. Sniff, sniff.

Am I imagining it?

No, for sure something *is* burning.

Holy Jesus! I know what it is. I must have left the iron on. And now it has burnt through the ironing board which ironing board has, in turn set the adjoining furniture on fire. Within a minute, the whole house will be ablaze! Holy cow! I must act quickly. Get bucketfuls of water and pour it on the raging fire. No. Better still, call the fire brigade. I quickly go to the phone and dial.

'Hello. Is-is tha- er the- fir-?'

Cows of my father! Am I trembling! I am scared *shitless*!

'Hello. This is the fire brigade. Is there a problem?'

'Of course there is a problem, you dim wit. Why else would I be calling you ?' I raise my voice. 'My house is on fire. Do you hear? FIRE!'

'Okay Madam, let's take it slow and easy,' the fireman says. 'Don't scream as though there is a Rion in the house...'

'What do you mean Rion?' It's now my turn to be surprised.

'Rion. The animal that eats people. King of the jungle.'

'Ah! You mean Lion?' Such a dim wit! Like many of us, this slow-thinking cop is a victim of first language interference where we don't have the letter L.

It can be quite embarrassing, this thing of first language interference. There is this man from the central region. The people of this region pronounce letter R as L. Our man goes to Europe for the first time. His host receives him warmly and soon they are at table having a warm conversation. His host asks him:

'So what is the main meal in your country?'

'Oh, we eat a lot of beans and of course plenty of *lice.*'

'Oh my goodness! *Lice*?" Exclaims the shocked host.

'Yes, many a time we eat *flied lice* and *kitchen.*' Fried rice and chicken.

'Well, it must be quite a *laborious* task to prepare a meal in your country,' the host stutters before choking on his food and collapsing in a heap on the floor.

Then there is this ex-guerilla chap, from the western region now a major or something in the army, who was explaining on a radio talk show why he joined a certain guerilla movement, after a rigged election.

'Erections were held and the erections were rigid, so we went to the bush.' The talk show host asked him to mind his language, adding that the listeners did not really care about his sex habits and whether the bush is a better sex venue than a bed.

Ah, and there was this teacher who asked his female student for his kiss.

'Go to my office and bring me the kiss,' he told the bewildered young girl.

Mad, the girl runs to the headmaster and reports sexual harassment.

The headmaster blows three fuses at a go and summons the teacher with intent to fire him on the spot.

With the calm of a bull that has been teased with a red cloth, the headmaster asks what the hell this man meant asking his student for a kiss.

The poor teacher took five full minutes to understand what was happening and then proceeded to plead his innocence.

'No, I never! All I did was to ask her to help me get my *keys* from my desk,' he pleaded.

The man, a Northerner, was merely a victim of his mother tongue and had no end of problems pronouncing certain syllables.

* * *

I was telling you about the call I am making to the fire brigade.

'Madam, where do you live?'

I direct him.

'We are on our way.'

At least he sounds as if he means it. Then he comes through again.

'By the way, Madam, are you *sure* your house is on fire?'

'What, you son of a he-goat!'

'Okay, okay. Sorry about that. We are on our way.'

Are you sure your house is on fire indeed! If the fool had asked me the question face to face, I would have given him some fire. For here I am, cocksure that I left the flat iron on, which burnt through the ironing board and sent the surrounding furniture ablaze. I can smell the pungent smoke and then this idiot has the audacity to ask me whether I am *sure* the house is on fire!

I look up towards the skies and ask the heavens to have mercy on this clumsy buffoon.

But one thing I have to give the fire brigade department: they are fast. I can already hear the sirens – loud enough to drown the sound of worship in heaven.

They are now here. As I throw open the front door, about twenty of them jump down from the truck ready with the water pipes.

'Madam, quickly show us the room where the fire is,' the leader shouts out.

'It is the third room down the corridor. I can't take you there because, unlike you, I have no protection gear.'

They all move in the direction I have pointed out.

'Halt,' the leader shouts. 'There is no need to proceed there. Just bring the equipment.'

Meanwhile, pandemonium has broken out in Village Eleven. The neighbours have all streamed out of their houses in different degrees of nakedness.

My immediate neighbour and his wife are not doing too badly – the man has no shirt, while the woman has a blouse on, but no skirt.

The two spinsters a block away come running to the rescue with such urgency, they only managed to put on their bathroom slippers and slip into the most transparent of all gowns with slits that reach the waist on either side. Actually two of the firemen ought to be charged with rape – what with the way they are looking at these two chicks! The Penal Code should introduce a crime like *mental* or meditated rape or something like that.

The widow in the opposite bungalow, who cannot be accused of dressing decently ever since her husband died, is making her point again. Two pretty boobs are peeping out of some excuse of a blouse she has on. At this rate we shall be one widow less, around these parts.

To be fair though, her husband died three years ago and she herself is still young. A widower would have remarried within a year or less. Our people believe and hold that a widower cannot live too long alone. Since he cannot look after himself and would therefore die quickly, he must remarry fast. But the widow? She is supposed to remain married to her dead husband! And the moment she casts an eye on a man she is called a harlot who can't wait to spread her legs!

One reason I have sworn never to sleep naked is because of situations like the one I am in just now. In the event that you went to bed in your birthday suit, in case of emergency, you look for what to cover your nakedness with but because of the panic, you will be lucky to find anything called a cloth.

'Hoist the hoses high now,' the in-charge shouts. He is a bull of a man. More like a mountain gorilla. You know like those ones in Bwindi impenetrable forest in western Uganda. Right physique for a fire fighter.

The two firemen who have not bothered to hide their impressions of the two spring chicken reluctantly obey their commander. Up the hoses go.

'Aim the hoses at the window now. Where you see the smoke coming from.'

It is done.

'Halt! Hold water,' he shouts again.

Silence reigns.

'Madam, *where* is the fire?'

'What do you mean where is the fire? I have already told you *where* it is. But it is apparent you have no fire in your belly. It is just full of shit, your belly.'

God, am I disgusted!

'Very funny. Now cut out the theatricals, woman; there is no fire here!'

'What do you mean there is no fire here? The iron which I left on and which burnt the-the-"

He looks at me strangely.

So do all the firemen and occupants of Village Eleven.

'Madam, I suggest you seek the services of a shrink.'

And with that, he gives the order for his group to depart.

'Seek the services of a shrink, my foot. *Shrink*!' I shriek. "Let me assure you, so-called commander of the Fire Brigade that it is you who is in dire need of those services. Fire fighting seems to have entered your faculties and deranged your mental capabilities.'

'Madam, under the circumstances, I should charge you for having brought us here on a false alarm. Ideally you should have paid for the fuel and time we have wasted. But because you obviously have a mental problem, the fire department will not charge you.'

Meanwhile the mountain gorilla of a man is actually looking at me with pity. *You obviously have a mental problem*! I can't stand it. I ca*n't*. For a fire fighter to look at me as if I have taken leave of my senses and actually *view* me as an object of pity!

'Depart!' The commander gives the order.

The way he shouts you'd think his troops are a mile away.

The firemen pick up their gadgets, load them on the truck and as they board, they all give me this strange look – except two of the firemen whose gaze still hasn't left my spinster neighbours. They will probably set a house on fire around here, just so they can return and look up these girls. The firemen are on fire!

'I think it is because her husband sleeps at that *other* woman's place most of the time. Now poor Liz is hallucinating,' one neighbour says under her breath, as the inhabitants of Village Eleven slowly make their way back to their homes.

I hear her. She is Nankinga, the village gossip, whose favourite pastime is minding other people's business for them.

We had enjoyed a brief spell of quiet ever since her boyfriend (the one before the one before the present one) spilled the beans. He had had to employ the services of a machete to chop a rather overgrown bush on either side of the river before jumping in for a swim, he told everybody who cared to listen. Then he moved on to what he said were cleaner and better waters, leaving a broken-hearted Nankinga too humiliated to peddle her tittle-tattle around the village.

I am embarrassed and enraged twice over. First, because obviously, there was no fire to begin with. Secondly, the advice of the headman to the effect that I should seek the services of a psychiatrist is true. And my wholesome shame has turned to immense anger.

That then is the level of madness I seem to be going towards.

Things reach a peak when the other day I put the shoe for the left foot on the right and vice versa.

It is like this: I am hurrying to go to office. Ishaka is busy blowing the car horn like one of those lunatics who drive Kampala taxis and shouting that I am making him late. I put on a pair of shoes and head for the car. Even before my bottom is square on the seat the car shoots off like a bullet, tyres screeching and chickens screaming. We set off in this pregnant silence.

Who is it that said it's easy to tell whether a couple in a car are husband and wife or lovers? The lovers will be busy laughing at nothing and everything. And trying to put zero distance between them inspite of the fact that they are on different seats. The keen observer will notice that the man's left hand is not exactly changing gears all the time; it has far more important concerns, as in roving all over the woman's thighs and going places we don't want to talk about here. The woman will not be complaining; this is one nuisance she will be only too happy to tolerate.

The husband and wife will on the other hand be trying their best to concentrate on the road; for some it is two perfect strangers who find each other an inconvenience they are still failing to get rid of. They both have fun elsewhere.

Anyways, I go to the office with the right shoe on the left foot and the left shoe on the right foot. As I enter the office, I notice people looking at me queerly. Holding their mouths in their hands and breaking out in giggles. I do not understand why.

'Madam, why are you walking like a duck?' The office *messenger* asks.

'Duck? What duck?'

'Duck. *Quack, quack, quack,*" she makes this irritating duck sound in this high-pitched voice that says louder than words that what a silly question!

I mean when it reaches the office messenger asking her boss – *boss* for heaven's sake! – why she is walking like a damn duck, then something *is* wrong.

I look down at my shoes and Jesus! Do I get embarrassed at the spectacle!

That incident heralds the beginning of a very trying time for me at the office. For the lower cadre in the office start bullying me mafia style. It's absolute torture. As soon as I step in the office, a myriad hidden voices start this song:

'Old MacOnald had a farm,
E, I , E, I ,O.
And on that farm he had some **ducks,**
E, I, E, I, O .
With **quack , quack** *here and quack* **quack** *there,*
Here **a quack,** *there* **a quack** *everywhere* **quack** *quack,*
Old MacOnald had a farm,
E. I. E. I. O.'

You should hear them when they come to the words *ducks* and *quack*. They are at their height of cruel sarcasm the lousy bastards. And the mocking laughter when they come to the grand finale of their accursed duck anthem. If they don't stop that crap, I know for sure that I will no longer have the courage to come to work. I think of reporting to the boss but I do not know who the hell the tormentors are!

And at the end of the tormenting anthem, they burst into almost inaudible giggles. Like hissing snakes, for heaven's sake! If I ever catch one of them *bas*tards, I will wring his lousy neck and feed his torso to the vultures that patrol our garbage-ridden city. I swear I will.

But it's not only these things that cause me worry. Anything to do with any slight illness sends me into a panic.

One day I feel this pain in my leg. It must be a blood clot. Good God! It must be travelling to my lungs at the speed of light! I am actually beginning to get this choking feeling. I can hardly breathe and I have started coughing! I dash to my doctor.

I reach the doctor's clinic.

'Doctor, I have got a blood clot!'

'Please. How do you know?'

'I know the symptoms. Pain in the leg, heavy chest, dry cough. Doctor, I can feel it travelling to my lungs!'

'Come and lie down here.'

He examines me thoroughly.

'You must have knocked your leg slightly on some object. This does not need any medication.'

Then I recall how I had tripped over this table in the sitting room.

Two days later, I get a bad running stomach. This was after drinking local banana brew from my uncle. This diarrhoea is unusual, with white floating objects, like giant jellyfish in the Sea of Japan.

Holy cow! How could I not see that this was pure cholera? I start panting. I am getting dehydrated! My tongue is literally hanging out of my mouth, in a way that a dog would find offensive, as a violation of patent!

Quick, there is no time to waste. I dash to the doctor like a rocket freshly launched.

'Doctor, I have got cholera – or something worse!'

'Slowly please, Liz! Who diagnosed you and which medical school did they go to – I should like to look at their transcript.'

'I know what cholera particles look like…'

At the end of the diagnosis, he declares me cholera free.

Another time, I get a boil under the armpit. My brow feels hot. I am in no shade of doubt what it is:

'Doctor please give me an injection quick, quick. I have got bubonic plague!'

He sighs, takes one good look at the boil that I am holding on to and says, 'This is no bubonic plague – unless you simply want it to be. You just have a slight infection somewhere.'

'*Where*?' I ask scared as hell.

'Oh don't worry. I will soon find out but it is harmless, nothing to dispatch you to eternity.'

It actually is.

Then a week after that, I notice some spots on my arm. What can this be? I keep on rubbing my arm though it is not itching. Then all of a sudden, I notice that the spots have turned some unhealthy yellowish colour, looking like half-cooked dry peas, the type you would only expect to find in a prison kitchen.

There is no doubt about it: it is smallpox.

'Please Liz. The world was declared smallpox free more than a decade ago!' The doctor says after my panicky entry into his clinic.

When I feel a slight pain on the right hand side, then it is cancer of the kidneys; any cough I straightaway think of TB; a headache means meningitis…

'Liz, you can't go on like this! Just burn all the medical books which you are obviously misreading,' Fina counsels.

Burn my medical books? She must be out of her mind! They are practically my lifeline! I get the biggest volume from the shelf. "All your Medical Queries answered" is the title. Quickly, I flip through the pages. Chapter thirteen. (Ominous number. A sure sign of grim things to come!) Yes, here it is. "How to tell when you are getting a stroke.' All the symptoms are here; pain in the shoulder (I have excruciating pain *there*), twitching of the right eye (mine is just doing a mad dance!), numbness in the left hand…

How dare Fina suggest that I burn all my medical books! How then would I have known about this impending stroke? Thank God for my medical books.

I dash to the doctor.

'You have the most normal heart south of the Sahara and north of the Limpompo,' he says after thoroughly examining me as relief floods through my entire being.

* * *

'I said good morning my dear,' the voice from the world of men brings me back to the present.

Ah, now. Welcome to Act One, Scene One. The one who has ruined my hard earned sleep is none other than the part time tenant of this home: the man whose name I cling to like a life-support machine. My dear husband, the author of my present ills, searer of my conscience, cause of all my misery, pursuer of my perils, the epitome of my dislikes and the personification of all that I now find objectionable, His Excellency, Ishaka.

'I said good morning my dear. Third time I am repeating it.'

'My dear!' Humph. He must have got his pronunciation mixed up. He probably means his *deer*.

And can you believe it? The fellow is actually whistling away merrily! As happy as a lark, if you please. After making his entrance at 7.00 a.m., for God's sake!

As if to increase my agony, he now switches to humming that popular tune by Chris Hinges that goes:

Envy me all ye that traverse the earth,
For I had the food of the gods for supper;
And oh glorious day!
I had sunshine for breakfast.

Oh how that tune makes me get emotional internal bleeding! Knowing as I do where he was for supper, bed and breakfast, such a tune is salt poured into a gaping wound.

I groan inwardly.

And the way he is stressing the *food of the gods* and the *sunshine*! He rolls the words around his tongue, obviously savouring them.

'Well, and why are you not answering me? Why are you looking as if you had *wasps* for breakfast?'

I grimace. So today's stars are predicting our diverse menus, are they? Well, mister, let me give you the menu that is lying on the tip of my tongue:

Ishaka, you come whistling merrily into our bedroom... Oh, did I say *our* bedroom? Pardon me. My bedroom is more like it. Because I can count on my fingers how many nights you have spent in it this year. And I can assure you; I do not count up to more than four.

Talking of fingers, reminds me of how much I mistrust you now. In the rare occurrence that we shake hands, I have to count my fingers to make sure that all five are there. For with you now, I am not sure of anything!

However, I am not telling you these things. Otherwise you will accuse me of being a perpetual nagger and then in this very judgemental voice, you will remind me that that is precisely why you got number two – a title which my spy network tells me Malai has refused. I am told that one day at a party, Ishaka, by way of introduction ventures 'please meet my second wife.'

Malai springs up in anger, bares her fangs and tells him 'never call me your second wife. I am your wife; do not number me.'

I have to quiet these things otherwise you will remind me for the hundredth time that you are fed up with the way I am trying to write another book of Lamentations.

But don't you worry your rather beautifully moulded head. I am not going to quarrel lest I send you scampering back to *her*.

So I dash to the kitchen and quickly get a glass of water from the pot. I can never drink water from the fridge – it is just too cold for me. (If I ever take water from a fridge, I first put it aside so that it can "cool" down to room temperature.) I then quickly take a mouthful, which I safely put in either cheek and close my mouth.

I will not spit out this water. For the moment I do, I might be forced to utter words which I may never be able to take back.

This is an old remedy I got from my mother. If you do not want to quarrel with your man, simply revert to that old trick of water in the cheek.

We all know that poor housewife who was never without a bruised face and battered bottom. She goes to a witchdoctor and complains that her husband never stops beating her, even for no reason at all.

The witchdoctor – a wily and crafty fellow – listens carefully and then gives her a parcel of herbs. 'When he starts using hot words put a herb into your mouth and chew on it – never answer him back; not a word from your mouth, you hear?' He asks sternly.

The woman takes the advice and returns six months later: not a single beating.

'You are the best doctor in the land,' she declares. The crafty old man smiles at his wisdom. He knows that as long as the woman does not bicker, the man can never, never touch her. All he had given was a simple medicine-less herb that could never cure the mildest headache.

'My dear, I thought I told you yesterday that we would be going to Kololo airstrip at nine. And then when I come, you are not ready. Why are you not ready?'

I stare at him.

'And what is in those cheeks anyways?'

He is beginning to get irritated. I can see it coming. He is knitting his eyebrows.

I only stare at him. Brother, you will not get a single word out of me. Except that my cheeks are beginning to hurt because of this damn water silencer.

'Well, what the hell has happened to your cheeks all of a sudden? When I came in, you were perfectly all right. Unless you have just been stung by a wasp. And it would have to be two wasps since the swelling is on both cheeks. An incredible thing if you ask me because two wasps could not have struck at the same time in the same positions. Not to mention that two different ones could have struck the same place.'

He turns this hugely suspicious eye towards me. But the blessed water is comfortably in the cheeks so I won't answer back.

He, heh, heh! You will not get a single word out of me. I have learnt the staring game and I can look at you for hours without batting an eyelid.

'Well, why the hell are you not ready?'

Oh yes. Indeed there is a big function at Kololo airstrip – the traditional venue for all major government functions. Whoever matters in terms of leadership in this country will be there.

Let me spit out this accursed water and tell you a word or two, you high and mighty husband in name, why I am not coming with you to Kololo. Should I aim the water missile straight into your uncaring face? No. I will be more civilised than you. Let me spit it in the sink. Phew! There.

'So my dear, why should I come with you for the function?' I ask in this voice, some 100kg heavy.

'Because you are my official wife. Simple.'

I laugh. Oh how I laugh. I laugh at you but I also laugh at me. It is a long time since I laughed like this. Yes indeed, laughter is the best medicine as the Reader's Digest calls it.

I can feel the stress inside me begin to melt. Oh, how good it is to laugh. I am enjoying the soft caress of the tears as they run down my cheeks.

'What is so funny? It is apparent that you have finally cracked up. I have always suspected that madness runs in your family.'

I keep on laughing indeed like a mad woman. I do not even have the breath to tell him that his own uncle was a proven night dancer and that this weird practice is genetic. So maybe he has a bit of it except it has not matured.

Neither do I have the breath to tell him that his maternal uncle used to *do it* with goats, sheep, cows and anything else on four legs that had any opening anywhere. Undisputed rumour had it that he was sexually allergic to any two-legged creature. So for him to think he is hurting me by alleging that I have inherited the madness of my clansmen is the joke of the year.

'My patience is wearing thin. Please put your act together so that we can go.'

Act. Precisely. For once in your lousy life, you have hit the nail on the head. That's exactly what going to Kololo with you would amount to: an act, a very big act. That's what our so-called marriage is: one big act.

I turn to him: 'You mean Malaika (flinch) cannot put up the same act? In fact a much better act than I ever could. If anybody knows how to act, then surely, *she* falls into the 'A' class. The superstar. She is in the same class with the *akina* Sharon Stone, Elizabeth Taylor, and those others we see in big movies. If she could manage to act her way into your life then, without any shred of doubt, she is one of the best actresses to have walked this earth.

'Is she not the best actress to have walked your stage? Strutting around you like a male turkey in advanced stages of a bad mood. That's why she has got you wired round her abominable arse. So why don't you take her, your Malaika, to Kololo instead of your *deer* old me?'

There. Her damn name is out. And I had thought it wouldn't escape from my mouth today.

CHAPTER THREE

OF NAMES

Getting that accursed name, Malaika from my mouth is as painful as a circumciser's knife. The fact that it is a beautiful name does not make matters any easier. In fact, it makes it worse. Her name is Malaika but I call her Malai because it sounds less beautiful. As matter of fact, to me it sounds a bit like malaria, the biggest killer-disease in Africa. And truly, Manga is the malaria in my life, except I will not allow her to decimate me.

You recall what our people say: that a bad name bewitches the owner? How I wish that Malaika horror had an ugly name! Then it would "bewitch" her. In any case, her name is her only redeeming feature.

Malaika. Meaning angel. *Angel,* for Christ's sake! It just makes me sick with jealousy. Because that's her damn name, I've gotten rid of all the records where the words Malaika or Angel surface. There is this beautiful one by the South African crooner, Miriam Makeba. Oh how I love it! *Used* to love it. Problem was that it turned out I was going to break almost all the records.

The most bizarre bit of my anti-Malaika disposition was the other day at a party with Ishaka. At midnight the DJ – who has all along shown plenty of sense – inexplicably loses his mind and plays Malaika.

Of course Ishaka is excited, drags me to my feet and before I know it I am on the floor, in his arms, no distance between us, Ishaka crooning along like a schoolboy in his first love affair. He is squeezing me like an octopus, his eyes glazed like one drunk on love. Then I realise that Ishaka is not really dancing with me. It is

Malaika that he is holding and dancing with, the bastard. I push him away and storm out of the dancing hall.

The fool remains stupefied, utterly perplexed. He does not realise why. A man who can't grasp what I feel this moment in time surely has porridge instead of a brain.

He is the kind of man who, during our most intimate moments, the stupid, selfish bastard will reach the top of the mountain and then scream out the wrong name. He will shout out Malaika's name instead of mine and not realise he has done it, or comprehend the damage he has meted out on me and whatever we are sharing.

I wish she had an old-fashioned name like Magdalene. This by any standard is a beautiful name. But because it is long, nobody would bother to pronounce it. You know the craze about abbreviating names – even though it is a manifestation of friendship to do so. People are always at pains to abbreviate even a name with three letters! There is this friend Tom. Which name is already an abbreviation. But can you believe that his family have further shortened the name to *To*? Ridiculous if you ask me. I mean this double abbreviation.

His wife has gone a step further – she calls him T. *T*! That's a triple abbreviation!

So Mangadalena (the vernacular equivalent of Magdalene) would be abbreviated to *Manga*.

Manga! Ha, ha, ha, ha!

'What the hell are you laughing at?' Ishaka asks with the politeness of a pig. 'Instead of you getting ready, you are busy laughing at nothing like a hyena."

Do you know, I had actually forgotten all about him and his Kololo trip.

'I am laughing at the name Manga.'

He looks at me incomprehensively, as if I have taken leave of my senses.

Yes, he would have tried to shorten the name. Then it would sound so ugly. Manga. This shortened name would also bring to mind *Mangasolfa*.

Did you ever taste it while you were still young?

The horrible medicine we used to be given for stopping diarrhoea or something along those lines.

Manga. It would sound so ugly: like something mangled. Untidy. Like mud, *dirty* mud. Manga.

MUD. He, he, he! How appropriate.

Something obscenely fat, very obese. As obese as those damn sheep I was counting when I couldn't go to sleep.

In the process of pronouncing it, his tongue would get entangled in his big mouth and then it would sound even uglier. The few occasions I have heard him say that wretched Malaika's name you would think he is rolling gold over his tongue…

'Please get ready. We *are* getting late.'

'Why don't you go with your Manga?'

I am gratified to see this look of utter stupefaction cross his face.

'And who the hell is Manga? Is that the new dog or something?'

That's a good one. I mean about her being the new dog. Yes, Manga is the *old* bitch around the corner. I must credit you with brilliant innovation my dear. You are spot on, on this one.

'Seriously, Ishaka, go to Kololo with Manga.'

'This only goes to prove my fears: that you are now a proven lunatic.'

I laugh again. Oh how I wish they had baptised her that in church. But knowing our churches, they probably would have refused to baptise her with *that* name. This is how it would have gone;

Reverend (Rev): Has this child *been* baptised or not?'

Mother: (Rev, I wish I could tell you that *that* is one of the most stupid questions ever been asked. Why *else* would these children be here for Christ's sake? You don't go looking for food unless you are hungry; you don't go to the doctor's just to say 'hello'. So what did you think we came here for, oh Reverend; to sip coffee?

You know very well that we brought them *for* baptism and you had already taken us through the procedure to be followed in the course of baptising them. So then why ask this obviously silly question?)

Rev: (With a trace of irritation in his voice) I asked whether this child has been baptised or not.

Mother: The child is not *yet* baptised.

Rev: Name the child.

Mother: Manga.

Rev: *Manga*! That is not a Christian name. It sounds like a *vernacular* name, therefore a *pagan* name.
That name is not acceptable. Give the child another name.

Mother: Etenge.

Rev: (With suspicion) What sort of name is that?

Mother: It is from Teso. It means hunger. The child was born during famine.

Rev: Well, there is no famine in heaven. That one is *definitely* a pagan name. *Please* name the child.

Mother: Kansiime. That's a *Kinyankore* name meaning praise Him (Jesus). That's *Christian enough,* isn't it?

Rev: Not at all. As long as it is not in English, then it is not a Christian name. To simplify matters therefore, why not name the child, Praise Him?

The mother tries to speak but nothing comes from her mouth. The white man must be smiling throughout his entire life. The African is the easiest person to brainwash. No wonder they colonised us – we were caught napping and engaged in staring at them like we were staring at the first wonder of the world. It is disgusting, I swear it is, that they come here and write stories about us. Like this professor whom I met at some University in Alaska. She comes and writes a book about some spirit medium in Uganda, a woman called Alice Lakwena. This Alice starts a rebellion against the ruling government in the late eighties. She gets together some rag tag army and tells them that if they smear shea nut butter on their chests, the enemy bullet will not kill them.

Instead, the bullet would boomerang to the one who had fired it and make him history. The priestess further tells her army that when her army throws stones at the enemy, the stones will turn into grenades and finish the enemy. Her army swallows this crap and goes ahead to confront a modern equipped army with nothing more forbidding than mere stones...

Oh Africa!

The well-trained army has a field day mauling the fools. It turns out stones can only be stones. Only one person – the Son of God – could ever have turned them into something else and even he decided that they do not have to become something different before they can accomplish the extraordinary. To Him, the stones could sing praises to the Lord if humans refused to. And the stones would do this while staying just as stony.

Oh yes. The way our people still think a white person is some kind of deity! It's like the other day when my friend comes to visit me. She comes with the four-year-old daughter of her neighbours, who happen to be Britons. She finds me with other visitors all of them grey-haired. We start chewing the cud. I tell the H.G. to make some juice and bring it for the visitors. It does not take long before she brings it and commences to serve it. She pours the juice into glasses and gives a glass each to the grey-haired couple seated near the entrance. She remains standing as she serves them. Then when she takes the glass of juice to the *four*-year old *Mzungu* girl, she *kneels* down for heavens sake!

* * *

Back to Manga's baptism. We are in church, remember?

Mother: Alright, Reverend, let me name the child.

Rev: Good. I am glad you are taking my advice instead of wasting further valuable time. So bring the child here.

Mother: But I have not *yet* got the English name you are so insisting on!

Rev: Eh, then we are talking at variance. I thought we *agreed* that you name the child *Praise Him*!

Mother: *Agreed?* (She flinches) I don't *know* about a*greed,* Reverend. This is ***my*** child remember.

Rev: Well, I did not think the child's parentage was under dispute. But anyway, go right ahead and name the child. However, remember none of your primitive pagan names again.

(Does he have to repeat it? The message has been clear enough even for the dumbest fool to follow.)

Her mind races with indignation, with the fury of a car being accelerated while it is in neutral gear. Can't we Africans have Christian names? Or are Christian names a monopoly of the white men; that if a name isn't "white" then it ain't Christian?

Are Charles, Godfrey, Geoffrey and the like Christian names just because they are English?

Who doesn't know that we too have our own Christian names?

We all know about that Great East African Revival that took place in the 1930s that swept western Uganda like a Noah-day flood. Since then the westerners indigenised the Christian names, giving African translations for Christian names – Mbabazi for Grace or Matsiko for Hope. Then they made up their own Christian names as well – that is why you see Tumwine (we have Him, Jesus), Twinamatsiko (we have hope) or Turyatemba (we shall go to heaven).

Thus it is not unusual to find somebody with both first and second names Christian, like Mary Turyatemba or Gideon Twinamatsiko and one of them a first and the other a surname. Or in the central region you will find Simon Mwesigwa (God is faithful) or Deborah Musasizi (God is merciful).

A big change from the times when kids were named mainly after seasons or landmark events. And we swallowed it hook, line and sinker. In some ridiculously extreme cases you find someone for instance called Peace Busingye! The two mean exactly the same. But still the white men think they have an unquestionable patent when it comes to Christian names!

Mother: The child is Heather, Monroe, Bill Clinton, Schwartznegger, Larry King.

Rev: Good. I name this child Heather, Bill Clinton, Swazi— Shwazy whatever—God ! I can't even pronounce the name! What does it mean anyway? But in any case, that is not the business of the church. *Feather*, *Monorovia*, *Bushy Clinton* Larry King *Live* and so forth, I baptise you in the name of the Father, and of the Son, and of the Holy Spirit. And I put on you the sign of the cross. Amen.

Mother: Reverend, please *unbaptise* my child. I will not allow her to take on those meaningless names. For all you know, maybe those names represent some foreign gods. I will take my child and baptise her myself. African names tell a story – to us at least.

Rev: Meaning*less* names? What do you mean meaningless names? What matters is that they are *not* pagan names. They are *proper* English names. Pure English. That's why I could not even pronounce them properly because I only stopped in primary *one*. But that does not mean I am stupid.

Mother: (under her breath) Well that is news to me. (Now loudly) But please unbaptise my child.

Rev: There is no such thing as *un*baptising a child. Once baptised, that's that. I have already put the sign of the cross on the child and *that* cannot be undone.

The mother snatches her baby and runs away from the Reverend and the church as if it is Lucifer himself after her.

The Reverend shouts at her or rather at her back:

'You have no authority to carry out the work of the church. If you so much as attempt to make the sign of the cross on that child's forehead, you will be excommunicated from the church.'

Excommunicate me?

Hew! Now, that's a tall threat. The mother is a convinced and practising protestant and does not want to be excommunicated from the church. Where would she go after being excommunicated? You know how our people are so steeped in religion that if the church disowns you, they look at you as Lucifer's sister. Or worse, Lucifer himself.

No. The mother does not want to rebel against the church. It is some of the so-called highly educated people who proclaim on rooftops, and proudly so, that they do not believe in God. Mercifully these are not too many. But in their heart of hearts, do you think that they really believe it? It is one thing to wear a façade of intellectualism; quite another when you sit down and get an honest opinion of you from you.

Nay. They just think that they sound cleverer and more modern and intellectually accomplished when they proclaim atheism.

For instance, there is this professor who has always proclaimed that he does not believe in God. Poor man. He has lost three of his children to AIDS. At one of the funerals the bearded professor painfully gets up. The mourners click their tongues sympathetically.

'Fellow mourners, I have always told you that I don't believe in God. Where is your merciful God? The one who is busy felling down my children? And this is the same God you call our Father, the most merciful? You should be ashamed of your hypocrisy.

"As for me, there is no way I can stand here at this hour when I am putting earth over my child and proclaim that: 'The Lord gives and the Lord has taken away therefore may His name be praised'! Not me. I simply do not believe in God. Full stop."

There is grumbling and murmuring. The people see this as pure blasphemy. Maybe that is why the professor is losing so many children, some say. No, that cannot be the reason, others say.

Because even those who are ardent believers are also losing their children.

At the end of his eulogy he says: 'May God rest my child's soul in eternal peace.'

A sigh of relief escapes from many of the mourners, while a murmur of 'silly fool' goes through a smaller group. The professor outwardly professes his unbelief in God, but inwardly he is a believer. It is in such moments that man's true self comes out, much to his shame, except that they seldom suffer the shame, since they are too busy contradicting themselves.

* * *

Names! Manga would definitely have escaped from being baptised with this name.

And talking of names, Ishaka has dealt me another blow in this avenue.

It is like this. God blesses our marriage with our lovely boy, Kirabo. Fortunately, Ishaka and I have been in agreement right from the word go that we will have two children. And our ardent prayer has been that we get a boy and a girl. So since we have a boy, our knees get sore as we keep on praying for a girl so that then we can call it quits. This is in the first six years of our marriage.

Apart from the reason above, I want a baby girl so that I can spoil her in her infancy. Girls look cute and there are so many things you can do with them to make them look so sweet. Frilled dresses, ribbons in their hair, beads in their braids...

Wait a minute. I used to love to see these smali girls with braided hair and multicoloured beads there. They just kill me. But the day I went to a hair salon and saw a small girl being tortured by huge women braiding her hair, I felt like calling the Chairperson of the Children's Rights Commission (does anything like that exist anyway? If not, somebody had better create it) to tell her to ban all braiding of hair of girls under twelve. This is the scenario at the hair salon:

Three women are seated on these cushioned stools. Seated on a mat somewhere between the legs of these women is a girl of about two and a half. Each of the women is busy pulling away at the poor girl's hair as they engage in endless gossip.

'Eh, have you heard? *Mbu* the other *ka*-widow is already moving out with your neighbour, even before grass has grown on her husband's grave.'

'What? I thought she was seeing the other man – what's-his-name – who drives a blue Toyota Carib.'

'*Sha*! How can such a pretty young thing sleep with that trash? The fool's tummy is so huge he can't see his toes. He has to stretch his arms full length and more, to scratch his stomach! You wonder how he would manage to do anything in bed, what with all that belly getting in the way all the time. The poor girl would go to bed hungry every night! Just reinforces my belief when looking for long distance runners you go for the smaller variety – ever wonder why it is always the smaller chaps who win the marathon?'

'You are moving your head too much, young girl. Please keep it in one position,' one of the tormentors orders the toy they are fiddling with.

'Girl, you have moved your head too far away from me. And don't sleep. If you sleep, we will spend two days on your hair. When you sleep, the hair kind of sleeps too and becomes impossible to braid. You understand?'

'Yes,' the girl says in a sniff. Obviously, she doesn't understand a thing.

'Like I was saying, my *co* (co-wife) is a horror. She wants the man every night. It is as if *down* there is constantly yawning for a prick. (Coarse laughter.) Girl, please don't move your head from side to side. I am about to lose my patience,' says the Amazon as she makes a twist on the braid and gritting her teeth, makes a cruel pull at the hair.

The girl breaks out into heartbreaking sobs and screams, 'Mummy, Mummmmmmy!' and the tigress actually puts her hand over the child's mouth! *Actually*! The girl buries all her molars into the cruel hand of her tormentor who gives a yelp of pain. She dare not slap the girl because if the girl reports it to her mother, it will become a police case.

The she-goat is frantically waving her wounded arm in the air, hoping that it will cool down. I applaud the girl by giving a hilarious clap.

'Bravo, young girl! Never take it lying down. You are a girl after my heart,' I hail her.

The three executioners all turn to look murder at me. I just laugh at them as I turn and get out of their torture chamber. I intend to make true my resolve to call the Chair of the Children's Rights Commission. If these kids' hair must be braided, a gentle way of doing it has to be found.

Do not get me wrong. I love braids – who doesn't? And oh how I wish many of our women in the rural areas and some of the poor lot in town could turn to braiding rather than perming their hair! Especially the straight and so called leisure curl.

Just go for a function somewhere deep in the village. You see these shiny hairs that look as if they have been smeared with mucus. Strictly nauseating. They look like spikes, some of these hairs. Others are brushed down and look like those of a rat fresh from the swimming pool – having, of course, fallen in by accident.

Whoever brought these perms to Africa has done us a disservice. Agreed the original African curly hair can be hard to comb but it *is* combable; you can run any comb through without too much chance of the comb breaking.

And whereas the more urbanite women folk can go to the right salons to perm their hair, our less fortunate sisters in the villages have to make do with all manner of so called beauticians who use even expired chemicals to treat hair. Then my mother-in-law the other day comes and tells me: 'You must give me money so that I can put *straighti permu* in my hair before I go back to the village.'

For crying out loud! She is over eighty! And whereas you might argue that age does not stop her from perming her hair, I still believe that in our context, such an old, rural woman should not put that poison on her hair.

* * *

Anyway I was telling you about this craving Ishaka and I have to get a baby girl. I get all sorts of advice on what I should do in order to get a girl.

'You know what they say,' begins my friend Fina. 'That if the man drinks a lot, he is likely to father more girls than boys.'

'How can that be?' I ask.

'Well, you know they say that when a man is drunk, his sperm travels a little bit slower than usual, kind of gently. He is not vigorous during the act, if you see what I mean. So the sperm goes slowly, gently upstream and the result is a girl. Whereas when he has sex when he is as sober as a judge (are they sober these days?) he shoots with all the energy in his body and the sperm results in a rough, tumbling boy.'

We both laugh. Knowing very well that that kind of story has its roots in people who started that nonsense of women being the weaker sex.

'So Fina, are you suggesting that Ishaka becomes a drunko?' We burst into laughter again.

'But you know what, Liz, you should try those herbal remedies...'

'Oh please! Both of us have got Masters degrees, for heaven's sake! How can an educated person like you talk like that?'

'Well you never know. And there is no harm in trying. It isn't as if you will be practising witchcraft. In fact, it is being illiterate to dismiss herbs as a primitive practice when you know that most of them are medicinal,' she insists.

I remain adamant. There is no way I can believe that herbs are going to determine the sex of a child. Until one day when I get a change of mind. This is what happens:

My uncle gets a problem very common among men of a certain age – he cannot pass urine.

After giving him drugs as a temporary measure, the doctor says he will pass urine for a while but eventually, they would have to insert a catheter, a very artificial and inconveniencing process for passing urine.

Fortunately, while in the hospital, somebody offers to introduce us to a specialist in herbal medicine who would definitely do away with the problem. But with our bias typical of modern, educated folks, we figure the man is babbling nonsense. As far as we are concerned, modern medicine is the one and only way out of this problem. We think there is no way the patient will survive an operation. If modern science could not offer a complete solution, we argue, neither could traditional medicine, dispensed by illiterate native doctors.

But somebody suggests that we have nothing to lose by trying and everything to gain, if it turns out well. We consent and the native doctor gives him a gallon of some yellow liquid whose name I don't care to ask, but whose performance turns out to be much better than its appearance.

If the colour is dull, the results certainly aren't. The first day he starts passing small quantities of urine. The second day is much better and by day three, he is doing it better than a pregnant cow.

That's all the proof I need. Living proof that our people ought to go back to nature instead of only banking on chemical stuff whose side effects are sometimes worse than the original ailment.

Yet another herbal miracle:

A woman known to me has a malignant cancerous lump in her breast, the perfect death sentence. A native doctor (some small chap with a wry smile and foul breath) gives her some powder from some herb, which she mixes with honey and eats for a few days.

Before long, the lady is bursting with good health and frolicking with the ease of a gazelle.

But there is a problem: unless you are used to taking this herbal medicine, some of these strange looking concoctions can be very difficult to tuck away. Traditionally, children are given herbs for all sorts of ailments and so they gradually get used to them. They sip them with the enthusiasm of one taking some good African coffee.

Problem, however, came when the born-again movement preached that taking herbs is tantamount to practising witchcraft because it was mainly the witchdoctors who were dispensing the herbs. So the born-agains refused to give their children herbs because they see it as a sin. In the early days, that is.

Recently, a cousin of mine who has grown up in one of the real puritanical homes gets a strong attack of fever while on a visit to our village. Naturally, the village folks recommend a herbal remedy known as *mululuza*, reputed for its ruthlessness in dismissing fever. After the first sip (a hesitant, cautious and experimental attempt), the poor girl throws up whatever she has eaten, and fails to take any more of the medicine saying it is *worse* than the fever!

"I'd rather die of the fever than of this dreadful stuff," she declares with a finality that entertains no argument.

In contrast, a little ten-year-old boy, also under a fever attack but who is accustomed to herbal treatment has no qualms about the issue. He quickly downs a cupful of the stuff and promptly asks for *more*!

A visitor who does not know what is happening can be forgiven for thinking the two have taken completely different liquids – one, a cup of bitter gall, the other, a bowl of sugared, warm milk.

Another lady is informed that some pharmacy has stocked a perfect herbal cure for the cervical cancer that is wasting her. Excited she rushes to buy the prescribed quantity of the stuff and proceeds to administer it. To her consternation, she cannot go beyond the first teaspoonful. The medicine, she says, is the most bitter thing she has ever tasted in her life. Worse still, it simply burns (yes, *burns!*) its way down her gullet and into her stomach making her wriggle and writhe like a woman in advanced labour. The sweat that results could as well be water from a broken pipe. In the end, she decides it is better to die of the cancer than of its purported cure.

The difference between the little boy and the two young ladies is that the former only manages the concoction because of adaptation, otherwise he would not have been able to take it.

So obviously, herbs have got their own problems. One of them being the bitterness in most of them. Maybe there is serious need to consider refining our herbal medicine so that it is more palatable to patients. For starters it could be made sweeter so that it is easy to swallow.

I consider all these things and decide that there is no harm in my taking herbal medicine in my earnest search for a girl child.

The following day, I visit a native doctor who starts giving me some concoction in five litre jerrycans. I drink it until I almost turn green! Truth be told, I don't know whether it is the herbs or the potions or just mother luck or a combination of all those factors that does it. Obviously I give the glory to God. When I conceive and give birth, out pops a baby girl – a raving beauty. She is a queen is my baby girl. Ishaka finds me in hospital and holds her lovingly in his arms.

'Eva,' he whispers lovingly in his daughter's tiny ear.

'What's that dear?' I ask. We are still in love and still call each other dear.

'Eva. That's her name. After my mother. The best way a man can show that he loves his daughter is to give her his mother's name. So Eva she is, will be. Eva the first woman, *original* woman. Woman 3.1.1.'

I smile with loving pride. Eva *is* a lovely name.

Four years after, Ishaka gets entangled with his Manga horror. Before long, she is pregnant. I privately hope she will gestate for two years like an elephant, but she somehow manages to keep it at nine and pushes out a baby girl. In a South African hospital! My spy network tells me that Manga tells Ishaka that she does not feel comfortable giving birth in our hospitals. And since he does whatever she wants, he buys two first class tickets to Johannesburg. This inspite of the fact that when I tell him I need money to fix our upcountry house, he glares at me and says he is broke.

Anyway, the *network* tells me Ishaka is all over himself over his new baby, kissing and cuddling her and calling her every endearing name I didn't even know existed. The way he is carrying on you'd think he has never had any child in his life! He is all over himself with excitement.

I am told that he even went with Manga to the labour ward, something that has not been happening around here. I mean the men usually stay at home or go to a watering joint when the wife is in labour. Many wouldn't think of going into the labour ward. It's like seeing his wife at her lowest moment, screaming and all. Well that's how it has been viewed anyway.

Few men ever want to see their favourite spot looking bloody and all messed up. They want to maintain in their mind that image of a clean, hairy rather than damp and bloodied environs. The moment that impression is distorted by a bloody mess in the labour ward, these silly sons of Adam will get turned off and stray to what they consider more pleasant precincts, sometimes for keeps. Of course they will never plead guilty as charged, but you long for the day when it will be all right to tether all men, to keep them from straying all over the place, eating whatever they find, without discrimination.

I hear Ishaka insisted on going with her to the labour ward, to hold her hand and bond with her. Bonding, my foot!

Really it is so unfair on my children. As far as he is concerned, they do not exist. They are like sheep with a delinquent shepherd, who leaves the sheep unattended in pasture and disappears to fill his liquor gourd – or empty whatever he finds there. There is very little space for them in Ishaka's life now. He used to mend things around the house with Kirabo. They used to find great companionship fixing this and that. Not any more. He has now abandoned this. When Kirabo asks for anything new, a pair of jeans or sneakers, his father tells him to wait until he is earning his own money which he can then spend on useless things like clothes.

Lost in my jealous misery, I decide not to follow the progress of father, mother and child. Until one day when the phone rings:

'Hello. This is Mrs. Ishaka. May I help you?'

'I would like to speak to Mr. Ishaka please,' says this woman's voice.

'I'm sorry Mr. Ishaka is not in. Would you like to leave a message?'

'Yes please. Tell him that Eva is very sick.'

My mother-in-law? But then, nobody ever calls her by her name!

'Which Eva?' I ask.

'His daughter,' comes the unhesitating answer with a tinge of impatience, the teacher attending to a slow pupil who is fond of asking the most stupid questions.

What the hell is this caller up to? Certainly *my* Eva is as fit as a fiddle.

'Look, Eva is in perfect health.'

'Madam, there must be a mistake. Eva is in hospital on drip!'

'Look here, whoever you are and wherever you come or are calling from, it is *you* whose head must be on drip.' Meanwhile I am looking at Eva playing outside, like a goat's kid, fresh from suckling.

'This is obviously a wrong number,' I say as I prepare to hang up.

'No please, Madam. This is Mr. Ishaka's home number. I mean this one you are talking on. I would not have called it if little Eva's life were not in danger. Madam Malaika, Eva's mother said to...'

I bang the telephone down hard, breaking one end of the receiver into several flying pieces. The lousy double-timing bastard Ishaka! After saying he was naming *our* daughter after his mother, he goes and gives the same name to his *other* daughter!

Of course this other girl is innocent but still am I enraged and deeply hurt! After all, isn't one entitled to righteous anger? At least there is no law against that.

CHAPTER FOUR

THE ENGINE

Incredible! Ishaka is actually busy strangling himself in the name of tying his tie. Lost in my thoughts, I had forgotten all about him. Funny that it is only one in 50 tie-wearers who knows how to knot a tie – whether correctly or at all.

'Well, when the hell will you get ready? We are getting late for heaven's sake!' Swearing is one of Ishaka's strong points.

'I am not going with you to Kololo.'

'Huh! Whom are you then going with?'

'Nobody. I am not going there at all.'

'And pray tell me why not?'

'I have already told you why I cannot go with you. I told you to take your *briefcase* Manga...'

'Oh please cut out that crap!'

I would have actually loved to go to Kololo. First, I believe it is important to celebrate such a day even though forty years down the road, after independence, few African countries can manufacture even a pin.

The other reason I want to go for those celebrations is to see many of the VIPs making fools of themselves. The M. C. announces the singing of the National Anthem. All those Honourables get up looking as patriotic as hell. But watch their mouths closely. Most of them know only the opening sentence of the anthem, which they make sure they sing out loud and clear. After that, you can clearly see that there is a definite discord between their lips and the words of the anthem. I mean if you have Honourable this one and Honourable that one and they don't even know half their anthem, then where the hell are we heading to?

And have you seen the mockery of these functions when they are held upcountry? The peasants are told to stand up and sing the National Anthem. In *English,* for God's sake! And so you watch these simple good village folk moving their lips meaninglessly up and down like misconstrued cartoons in a badly produced comedy.

Why can't these Honourables see that the national anthem should be translated in our local languages so that the people can feel part of it and understand what they are singing about?

'But a National Anthem should only be in the nation's official language which in our case is English!' Some official reasons one day when I confront him. What crap!

"Please get ready." Ishaka's voice brings me back to the present.

Don't you worry my brother Ishaka. I will get ready.

I will come with you to Kololo Ishaka, for I know how important it is for you to be seen with me. But I also must admit that it is equally important for me to be seen with you.

You must cut the picture of a responsible family man. And I must cut the picture of a happily married woman. Ahaaa! Such is the world. Sorry. Such is the African situation. This is not Europe where people divorce over a difference of opinion about small matters like the colour of a fly. I recall this story about a couple that argue about the whereabouts of a newspaper. The wife says it is in the upper drawer while the husband says it is in the lower drawer. But none of them can locate in which drawer the said newspaper is. Eventually the H.B. finds it. The wife insists that it had been in the upper drawer while the husband insists on his earlier stand. They argue for days on end and eventually break out into a near fatal physical fight. After several months of this domestic war, they decide they cannot stay together any more and opt for a divorce, which they go ahead and get. Funny that our friends that side of the earth divorce faster than they marry.

After one year, they accidentally meet in a pub. They sit and are soon chewing the cud on this and that. After which they realise that they are actually in love and had never been out of it. They take a decision to remarry and consequently have a glorious wedding. They live in marital bliss for more than a year. Then one morning as they are having breakfast, the husband looks deeply into the eyes of the wife and quietly says: 'My dear, you can imagine how many marriages break up because of very flimsy and very stupid reasons. See how we almost lost each other over a very silly argument. We must have been mad to separate over the whereabouts of a mere newspaper. You can imagine: that newspaper was in the upper drawer and yet we went on and on arguing about its whereabouts.'

The wife frowns: 'No. But it was not in the upper drawer. It was in the lower one.'

'Now that's really stupid. You know very well that it was in the upper one,' he replies in a raised tone.

And the argument starts all over again and soon degenerates into a bitter quarrel.

It does not take long before the snarling couple starts throwing any object they can lay their hands on at each other. And the process for a second divorce is soon underway...

* * *

'Well, are you getting ready?'

Back to the present, again. I laugh inwardly. I can imagine what those people who know you and me and Manga will think when they see us together.

You see, I am much more beautiful than your Manga. Starting upstairs, down to the dairy section and down to the transport department, I am definitely much better endowed than Manga. I am a woman that people will look at and say: there goes a beautiful woman. Mind you, I am not claiming to be a head turner neither would I have won a beauty contest in my hey days. No, I do not halt the traffic on city streets, but I am comfortably beautiful.

But Manga! She is decidedly ugly. And it's not because I am jealous of her. I have tried to look for some redeeming feature on her and failed to get a single blessed one. Ugly is her middle name. Without any shade of doubt, she would win the Miss Universe Ugly Contest. Goats on tether will break free from their ropes when they see her. Seriously, she is *that* ugly.

She will halt traffic and heads will peep out of car windows and people will click their tongues in sympathetic disgust and say: God! That woman sure is ugly. Her face looks like a complicated road map.

Ishaka, just take another look at her head. It looks like that of *Sebaddu wobuwukka* (the chief of ants)! This monstrous head has got twin peaks that will compete with Mt Everest. In between these peaks are deep gorges, which have enough space for a river to flow through. How on earth could you have picked on anybody with a nose the equal of which can only be the snout of a pig? And when she is around you, does she leave any oxygen for you? My dear Ishaka, one of these days, you may die from lack of oxygen!

Her bosom is another story. She has this obscenely huge bosom, with flat breasts touching her flabby, caterpillar-segmented abdomen. Whenever she laughs, her abdomens shake in a jelly-like fashion.

Younger than me though she be, she looks twice my age.

Manga looks like a poorly constructed scarecrow that would not only keep the birds and monkeys away from your garden, but would promptly silence all the crying kids in the neighbourhood. Because the bottle is never far from her lips, all you see is a haggard face, transparent cheeks with the flesh already folding like that of a grandmother baboon, eyes unfocussed and with a glassy look.

You could use her legs to pick your teeth! It's a wonder how such spindly legs can support the likes of her huge torso. But like our people say, an elephant cannot fail to carry its tusks.

Which brings me to my most agonising problem; for Manga's ugliness is my public undoing.

For when a man abandons a decidedly beautiful, well-educated (I have a Masters) woman like me for a decidedly ugly, less educated (she has one degree – not bad anyway) one like Manga, wagging tongues jump to one conclusion: the intruder must be in possession of a better *engine* (I hate the way they use that word. Engine indeed!) than that of the wife. Better a live dog than a dead lion, the Bible says. Could this be coming true in my own life?

Otherwise, what else could have attracted the man to her? And when the wife happens to be well-behaved like in my case (true story), this strengthens the rumour further. Because indeed why should a husband look away from a beautiful, well-behaved wife for a less beautiful (ugly in Manga's case) and not so well behaved (Manga is the definition of bad manners)? All rumours then run towards the accursed engine of the new entrant.

Then they start saying with this all-knowing wink: you never know what makes a person fall in love with an ugly one.

I will tell you this: whoever coined the saying that beauty lies in the eyes of the beholder must have had the likes of Manga in mind. The founder of this saying more probably than not wanted it as an apology for those in Manga's category.

Then when matters reach that level, the sex bit, any reasoning flies out of the window. Believe you me, when sex comes into any argument everything else gets forgotten.

And for the 'original' wife, your self-worth evaporates when everyone around you starts whispering that her *goods* are better than yours. Or that they are *packaged* much better. And how I hate that word *goods*! As if they are on *sale*! Makes you think of market stalls.

It torments me to think that, actually, the reason Ishaka went to Manga could be because she has a better engine than mine. It torments me so much that I confront Ishaka one night. I have been waiting for him. It is after midnight and I am still waiting. Then I hear his car in the drive. Quickly, I throw off my clothes. I switch on all the lights.

He comes in and registers shock at my naked exhibition.

'What's the matter with you? Have you taken leave of your senses?'

Meanwhile I stand with legs astride:

'Ishaka, I want *you* to tell me what the matter is with me!'

'Just remember that you are a mother of two and stop scandalising yourself.'

And with that, he slams the bedroom door with a bang thereby slamming the topic closed.

But does Manga actually have a *better* engine than me?

Does she? I doubt it.

For in our culture, what constitutes an excellent *engine*?

There is this thing of *pulling*. Pulling the *genitalia* to elongate them and keep the environs warm for due consumption.

Brother, in some cultures, if you have not pulled, you are considered half a woman. In some cultures, a girl may even fail to get married if she hasn't pulled!

Nobody has ever found out the exact merits of this pulling. Before Ishaka proposed to me, he asked: "Incidentally, love, have you *pulled*?"

As if pulling those little things down there makes any difference to the quality of the whole woman. But again, like the Good Book says, it is the little foxes that spoil the vines.

There is nothing incidental about his question. As he asks it, there is this note of deep anxiety and something akin to fear in his voice.

'Well, *have* you?' He asks as he literally holds his breath. He is waiting for the answer as if his entire life depends on it. Maybe it does.

'Yes. I have.' And his breath whistles out with obvious relief. 'But tell me, what does it matter whether a girl has pulled or not?'

'Well, it gives the man pleasure.'

'What *sort* of pleasure?'

He scratches his head and looks uneasily around. There is this silence as I look into his eyes searching for an answer.

'Well?' I prompt.

'Well-er- you see and you know,' he fumbles for words, like a kid who can't explain the sugar on his lips.

'I don't *know* anything.'

'Well you see it is like this. I mean it is *like* this.'

When somebody starts shopping around for words, then they don't have a convincing reason or they are about to tell a lie.

'It is like *what*?'

'Thing is, a man *kinda* feels nice, *sort* of good when he touches *them*. I mean them *pulled* things. I mean they make a man feel *sooo* good, like he is on top of the world. I mean.'

Hmm. When someone repeats *I mean* so many times or *kind of* or *sort* of, he is telling a lie or simply making up the story as he goes along.

'And you see...ah...these things are kinda psychological or somethin'...' he adds.

'As in?'

'Well, it is like this.' Again!

'Er – for instance, these waist beads that some women wear. See, they make the man happy. Like you know when he touches them and they make this soft music – *sort* of music anyway. He feels good, does the man.'

'I will never put those silly beads around my waist!' I declare. "Suppose the string breaks as I am walking on the street and them beads fly all over the place? Or suppose this happens as I am walking down the office corridor?'

'Well, that is what are called professional hazards. But it is really entirely up to you. But as our people say: *Otamanya ekimutungire eya iba agikwatisa gumwe*' a woman who does not know her lifeline holds her husband's penis with one hand.

I have got his drift. This *pulling* thing or the beads issue are only there to enhance the man's pleasure like in massaging his ego.

It's not that it will give him added physical pleasure. But if the woman has *pulled*, then it means she did so to please a man. If you have *not* pulled, then it means that you do not accept man's superiority. You are not paying homage to him and acknowledging him as supreme leader, somebody whom you must please!

How enslaving! Must woman always pander to man's whims? That ultimately means that woman has accepted the label inflicted on her by society: she is above all, just a sex object - from the men's point of view..

Spending precious time as a girl out in the bush and making sure no prying eyes see you as you pull.

You are advised by an Aunt to *pull* before you have your first blood; when your skin is still tender. Otherwise after that, your skin will harden like the hide of an old cow. Then trying to pull it will be like trying to elongate a piece of metal. Time is suspended as my mind travels back into time…to the time I *pulled...*

* * *

I am ten years old. I have not yet seen the moon. My Aunt has already told me to get in touch with a cousin who will tell me what to do. She comes one evening, my cousin Mera.

'Come and we go to the well,' she says.

'It's getting late,' I tell her.

'Come on, people are still moving,' she says.

I get my pot and we quickly run to the well. Water wasps are swimming in the well.

'Quickly, catch one!' Says Mera.

'I can't! It will sting me!'

'That is supposed to be the purpose – to sting you. Except not to sting your *fingers* but your ...'

'My *what*?' I ask, scared as hell.

'Your breasts.'

'My *wh*at? You must be out of your mind,' I shout already feeling a slight pain in my small budding breasts as if the wasp is already stinging.

'Well not your breasts as such. Your nipple.'

'*Nipple*? You must be out of your mind!' Indeed she must be.

'No I am not. Look cousin, when the water wasp stings your nipple, your breasts grow within no time and look like an orange. If you do not apply the wasp sting, your breasts will sag in the nearest future and no man will want to marry you. They will look like those of an old woman. See?'

I see all right. She gets the slippery wasp from the well and puts its mouth at the tip of my now exposed nipple. I close my eyes tightly and wait for the pain.

'*Ouch*!' I scream.

'Not so loud. Otherwise somebody will come. Moreover, that was no pain. If you are scared of that small pain, then how will you push a child?'

I keep quiet.

'Now, let us go behind that bush,' she says as she leads the way. Meekly, I follow like a lamb going to the slaughter.

The bush safely hides us.

'Now then, take off your pants,' she commands.

'What?' I exclaim in shock.

'Stop wasting time. It is growing dark and we have to do it while there is still light.'

'Do *what*?'

'Pull. What's the matter with you? This is why we are here. Operation pull. Just take off your pants,' she commands with impatient irritation.

Somebody to see me naked! I am at the height of embarrassment. But Mera is giving me such an eye, I just find myself removing the pants.

'Now open your legs wide.'

'What?' I shriek.

Then she goes into action. She flings my left leg here and the right one there.

'How else will I show you *where* and *how* to pull?'

Oh, the shame of it all. I am very sure Mom would not have approved. This must be demonic, evil.

'These are the two areas you keep pulling at until they are long. It will take about two months. Do it like this, like this.'

Meanwhile she is at it, like she is *milking* a cow.

'You use these special leaves, the *entobo* leaves. You don't use any and every leaf that comes your way,' she says, as she milks away with the ease of a practised milker.

'When you get married, you will remember this evening and be eternally grateful to me.'

My mind is preoccupied with this shame that is taking place between my legs. I don't care what happens years after.

'Now we can go back home. Tomorrow you will be a little sore. But give it two to three days and it will fade away. Then you can start pulling again after that.'

Tomorrow you will feel a *little* sore! What an understatement! I feel *so* sore the following day that I can hardly walk! I walk with my legs apart and Mom soon notices.

'What happened?' She asks with suspicious concern.

'An- acc- accid- an accident,' I end on a lame note.

'Let's have a look.'

My heart is pumping. Mom is a born–again Christian. I am sure she frowns at such shameful practices like the one which caused me to walk with legs wide apart like a lame duck.

She makes me lie on my back and tells me to remove my pants. It seems a woman is destined to spend her life removing her pants for reason A or reason B or all of them reasons!

'Ah I see. You did that thing. That's all right,' says Mom after examining me.

Then she pauses. Looks thoughtfully into space. *It* is coming, I think fearfully. When she said it is all right to pull, she was only preparing me for the stinger to follow.

'But child, never strain yourself over such things like *pulling* if you don't feel like. They are just things of the flesh. *Outward* things.

Things that can be cut off and you remain intact, you remain yourself.' She pauses again, looks into space, and then gives this heavy sigh as her eyes come back into contact with mine. Our souls touch during this minute that seems to go into eternity. It is the umbilical cord story once again, the one knot that even though severed at birth can really never be severed.

'At the end of the day, it is the *you in you* that matters.'

And she gives me her gentle, reassuring smile. Does Mom. My breath whistles out in relief as I rush into her arms and she holds me close to her breast...

After four days, the soreness is gone and I am not sure whether or not I should resume *operation pull.*

Mera however decides for me.

'Well, have you resumed?'

'Ah...er...er... not really.'

'What do you mean not *real*ly? You either have or you haven't. And from the look of things, you haven't.' And she gives me this accusing look. Jesus! It is as if I have committed the *original* sin!

'Look here, don't be silly. This is your only opportunity. I told you that if you wait until you get your period, you won't be able to pull because your skin will be as hard as that of ...'

'Okay, okay,' I hold up my hand for her to stop. I don't want her to repeat the stuff about my skin being as hard as that of a crocodile or somethin'. I hate it when a person keeps on repeating that kind of crap. It gets on my nerves. It takes away even my reserve nerve.

'I will resume pulling.' Ceasefire. It's fine to resume. After all Mom has said it's alright to pull, especially if you feel like it. Why is Mera bothered about my pulling more than I am, anyway? Talk about crying more than the bereaved.

'As I told you, it is for your own good. I mean why should I go out of my way to persuade you to do it? It is because I am not selfish. Another malicious person would keep the sacred information to herself.'

She has read my mind to the letter. She is not as dumb as I thought she is.

'Yes, this is what this information is: Gold. Sacred,' she is saying.

Sacred? So that's what it is, or is it? But she is probably right or why should she go out of her way to make sure I go through with the project. I mean about her not being selfish and all. For indeed why should she care? But on the other hand, it could be that she wants me bonded the way she has been. You know how it is. It could be like some kind of *club* – you make sure you recruit as many people as you can. Some kind of *cult* if you see what I mean even though I am not sure *I* know what *I* mean.

'Incidentally, I pull until they are how long? I mean them things. I pull until they are how long?' I ask Mera , the expert. The *consultant*.

'The *longer* the better. Men like them that way, my aunt says. There are women who have them so long that when they go to the latrine, they have to carry two pieces of saucers on which to *place* them so that they do not come into contact with the unhygienic surroundings.'

'Mera!' I exclaim in shock.

She only laughs at me.

Anyway, I pull the stuff until they elongate so much that they dangle between my legs.

But not too long though; I have to stop when I hear of this woman whose husband fled on their wedding night, screaming that he had married a fellow man, except that he had *two* penises. It turned out the girl had been so enthusiastic at pulling, she ended up with her stuff so long, the man took one look at them and decided there was no way he was going to sleep with a woman who had a penis, let alone *two*!

I think it a little funny that while we are busy pulling ours so hard, our friends in the mountains of the east are chopping them off, saying their men like it that way! Do men ever know what they want? How can two groups of men in the same land, look at things so differently?

* * *

And so pulling or not cannot be the secret to holding on to a man. Manga herself tells me so to my face, the bitch, when I confront her in a hotel.

Fina tips me that Ishaka and Manga are in The Parasite Hotel, at a time when their love affair is at fever pitch, before they get their customary marriage. *Parasite*! How appropriate.

'Go and give her a hiding. She shouldn't just walk in and snatch your man without you putting up a fight! You are not a saint, for Christ's sake.'

I don't need further prompting. I head for the damn hotel. Fina even knows they are in room No.44. She is that thorough.

'And if you need a back-up force just ring me,' she offers. I smile gratefully.

I reach the hotel and start looking for the goddamn room. Here it is. I knock discreetly. My heart is in my mouth.

I am about to knock again but I hesitate as a whirlwind of ideas rush through my mind. Suppose Fina was wrong? What if Ishaka and Manga only came for a cup of coffee?

I laugh at myself, because I know I am wallowing in self-deception; behaving like the reporter in a story I once came across.

There was a prominent leader who was having a nice little affair with someone's wife. If it was nice it had to be someone else's wife – *awalungi tewaba wammwe* (the really nice place is never your home). So the editor of a newspaper calls his reporter and tells him he had whiffs of evidence – nothing too concrete yet – that the philanderer was due to meet the unfaithful woman at a certain residence. And they were not just going to sip coffee. Maybe a little more than that.

'Go get the story,' said the editor. The young man goes off for his assignment as the editor licks his lips in a way that would make the cats invoke the Patent Act, in anticipation of a scoop that would make headlines the following day.

Big story. Big money. More popularity for the paper. You can imagine how deflated the balloon was when the young man showed up with no story.

'What happened?' The editor was flabbergasted.

'I took position from a certain window and saw the couple walk in,' the young man began.

'And then...?' The editor was impatient.

'Then they started kissing passionately,' he continued.

'Of course it had to be passionate; get to the point, fellow.' The older man was now unable to mask the fact that his impatience had turned to irritation.

'Then they started removing their clothes...' This time the editor poked the young man's ribs to quicken the narrative.

'Then they entered the bedroom...'

'So how dare you say you have no story you little bastard, when you saw them entering the bedroom naked?' The editor boomed, spittle flying freely and the voice echoing down the rest of the building, now largely deserted. Thunder couldn't have done it better.

'Problem was that they switched off the lights and I could not see anything; that's why I couldn't write a story.'

The room got deathly quiet for five minutes as the big man lowered his head slowly, like a station signal motioning for the train to enter, and fixed his gaze steadily on the floor as though he would never look up again.

He had waited a long time – it was coming to midnight – to get this story and here was this insolent puppy who had carried his tomfoolery from his father's compound to the workplace.

'Young man,' the editor took off his glasses, laid them on his table and clasped his hands like a teacher talking to a really dumb kid who only understood after days of explanation. "At that point any reporter worth his salt needn't have seen anything more in order to write the story. After a couple take off their clothes, walk into a room and switch off the lights, what do you expect?

'Did you think they were going to recite the rosary or pray for the king's good health?'

So it's like me now. Should I really think Ishaka and Manga are in the room praying to some god or discussing the millet harvest?

* * *

Finally I knock again at Room 44.

'Who is it?'

Ishaka! God! It *is* true then. I had hoped that I would find that my friend had made a grave error.

'Room service,' I say in this soft voice. Trying to sound as professional as hell. I mean as a professional waitress.

'Hold on,' he says loudly. 'Just a minute honey,' he adds softly, his voice love – no, lust - laden.

Honey! God, should I have come to listen to *this*? It's killing me! Already. I close my eyes in agony. His hand is now on the doorknob and I prepare to pounce on Lot's daughter. This Lot in the Bible. You remember how the entire city where he, Lot, lived was morally rotten. Including his own daughters who wanted to defile him!

Yes, I will show Manga something that will teach her not to tamper with people's husbands.

The doorknob is now turning. Then there is a pause.

'But come to think of it, we didn't order for anything!' Then in that lust filled voice he adds: 'Did we, darling?'

Honey. Darling. All said in this almost inaudible voice. As if he is addressing a baby whose eardrums he does not want to injure with a loud voice. The last time he addressed me with those endearing words was during Monica's wedding. Eight years ago, to be exact. He might even go to the extent of calling her *baby*! Sometimes it gets ridiculous when adults start calling each other baby! There was this megalomaniac of a giant who ruled Uganda in the seventies. It is reputed that he used to insist on his mistresses calling him 'baby'. Baby indeed! *Some* baby. This buffoon of a president is reputed to have eaten one of his children. Somebody argued that it was not true the man ate his child, as he only ate the kid's heart or liver. But then I wondered what is left of a person after you have eaten out their heart or liver!

Anyway, story has it that some highly knowledgeable witchdoctor advised him that if he ate the liver (or was it the heart) of his favourite child, he would rule forever. That seemed a perfect panacea to the power problem of the then Africa's top megalomaniac. Like people of his type, he trusted only two people: the first was himself and the second was of course, not you; so any advice was welcome. Calmly, we hear, he slaughtered one of his sons, ate his liver and/or heart and drank his blood. As it turned out, he lost both son and seat.

Now, now. This is the same baby eater who wants to be called baby!

Back to the action at Parasite Hotel.

Ishaka is asking Manga whether they have ordered something to eat.

'Not anything I can think of, sweetheart. We have enough of ourselves to eat anyway.' And then follows this heavy, lust-filled laughter of lovers.

God! Why did I come? Is this not the height of self-torment?

But I have to carry the onslaught to the end. The jealousy, the anger and the hurt I feel give me courage to tenaciously dig in. I take another shot.

'You had ordered for break...' Shit! I don't know whether to say breakfast or break tea! It's way beyond either. But knowing that they must have been too engrossed with themselves to order breakfast, I give it a long shot.

'You had ordered for a late breakfast,' I say in a firm voice.

'No thanks a lot. We have already had an early and late breakfast. Haven't we darling?'

The answer of the wizard is lost in giggles and a loud kiss, which smothers her mouth, I am sure.

Oh, oh. Will I survive this pain? It is obvious that they are giving each other *doses* of TLC – Tender Loving Care.

'All right. So sorry. I will take back the breakfast.' My mind is racing to find another way in which I can gain access and beat Manga into pulp.

'Hey you! What the hell is wrong with you? You mean you are *still* there? What sort of waitress are you if you can't even read? We put a clear DO NOT DISTURB sign. You should be sacked. Now fuck off. We are on our honeymoon, for heaven's sake!'

Honeymoon? *Honeymoon*! Then all of a sudden, something within me snaps. It is called cutting wires around these parts.

'You lousy sonofabitch, stinking bastard! I will give you a honeymoon you will never forget. Cat, dog, hyena, despicable rat. And that common whore. Cheapest harlot ever on the market. Open the door and I will show you where you came from, lousy bitch.'

I am shouting, I am screaming. I am kicking the lousy door. I am out of myself. Another being has taken me over.

Within no time, the whole damn hotel staff have arrived at the battlefront.

'Madam, please stop. What is happening?' The manager asks.

'None of your business. This is domestic,' I throw at him.

'Madam, it cannot be a domestic issue since it is taking place here at the hotel premises,' he asserts.

'This is not a hotel. This is a brothel. A flesh market. A bodyshop. This hotel reeks of fornication,' I spit back.

'Madam, this is one of the most respectable hotels in town and...'

I laugh like a maniac. I am demented.

'*Respectable* hotel? Respectable hotel, my arse. It is as respectable as Sodom and Gomorrah! Respectable indeed. Respectable hotel that is a rendezvous for whores and the men whom they have lured away from their wives! Anyway, get out of my way and I finish this Jezebel.' I am likening her to this woman in the Bible who lured King Ahab into sin and idol worship. I aim a deadly kick at the door.

'Open you damn adulterer!' My foot is bleeding but I don't give a damn as I aim another deadly kick at the stupid door that won't break.

'Please madam, calm down. You are spoiling the name of the hotel and ruining our business. Please allow me to escort you out of here.' And the bastard is actually putting his lousy hand on my arm, propelling me along.

'Spoiling the name of the hotel and ruining your business? That's a good one now. Like hell I am. Your hotel is nothing but a home-breaker.

'Let go of me, you manager of illicit trade. You are part of this. An accomplice. It is you who gave them the premises and so you are as guilty as they are,' I say as I push him away. 'And you harlot in there with my husband, how can you ever think you are better than me when you never *pulled*? Yes, I know it: you are nothing down there. You are naked, not a woman because you didn't *pull*. No man can love you. You arc cmpty, an empty granary,' I shout triumphantly.

I have got undisputable evidence that she *never pulled*. Her former best friend told me. They fell out on account of the fact that Manga started boasting that she had hooked a rich guy. She was talking about Ishaka. Her best friend eventually felt disgusted the way Manga was always talking about the things she had done with Ishaka. So the best friend crosses to my side and spills the beans about her former friend. All. The beans I mean. Maybe some of it is spiced up information but who cares? Certainly not me.

Then Manga, still inside the hotel room, breaks out into this loud, cynical laughter. I wonder what the goat is finding so funny but I don't have long to guess the source of her uncalled-for mirth.

'Liz,' she begins.

'Don't you dare *Liz* me!' How dare she call me by my name? The hyena.

'I pity you.' She continues as though she didn't hear me. 'How can you stand out there and say no man can love me because I never pulled? It's true I did not pull. But in spite of that, I am here in bed with your husband am I not? And you who pulled is out in the cold!'

Checkmate! I am stunned. I don't know what to say. I look helplessly around. It is actually very cold. I feel very chilly all of a sudden, but it is a bit too late to make a graceful and dignified exit.

'Shut up, you old cow!' I say lamely. There is no fire in the statement, just cold, impotent ash.

But I mean I had to say *something.* I just couldn't keep quiet could I? Except if you are to make a counter attack, it should be a strong one, not like the feeble one that has just started from my mouth.

'Madam, please let us leave. You will hear many more things that will hurt you real bad,' the manager says, pleading.

The warthog, porcupine and all that type of thing hears the Manager's advice. She takes up the cue:

'Why don't you just go home like a good wife and look after your children instead of trying to trail your husband?'

'Spare me your lousy advice, porcupine. How dare you presume to advise me?' I charge.

She ignores me. It is as if I have not uttered a word.

'And one other piece of advice. If I were you, I would never mention those things you pulled. I am talking about those hanging pieces of flesh you carry between your legs. I thought you were clever enough to know that what matters to a partner is what *you are;* the real you, not the additionals which you have put on your body.'

'Don't try to be wise. You can never be with that head of yours with *posho* for brains.' *Posho* is the meal made from maize flour.

God! Am I enraged! I am even more enraged because she is telling me a truth which Mom told me more than thirty years ago: 'What matters is the *you in you.*'

* * *

'Madam...' the voice of the manager brings me back to the present, his hand on my elbow gently probing me along.

But Ishaka's bitch is not yet done with me.

'By the way, those pieces of elongated flesh you carry along between your legs like two cold *dead* lizards, don't you think you should have them amputated since they have obviously been useless to you? It is apparent that they have not served the intended purpose,' and she breaks out into loud, callous and cackling laughter, the one the devil reserves for when he gets another soul in hell.

I feel *them* things sort of move uncomfortably. They are sensitive. Very sensitive and recoil into themselves when abused. They too get stressed. Anyway inspite of what she is saying I'm kinda happy I've got them. I feel a complete woman; one with whom a man should have no quarrel in this regard.

I think quickly. I must say something to neutralise her last sting.

'You can cackle...' I begin only to be interrupted by the Manager.

'Madam please don't listen,' he is saying.

'Let me tell you, toad, you will never have my man for keeps. For I have got his ring. We are married in church, which you will never be. You will never have his ring.' I end on a note of triumph as I twirl the ring finger proudly around. It is as if she can see it. There. Gotcha now. This will compensate for the loss I suffered in round one.

She croaks – the noise she makes is supposed to be some kind of laughter. But I tell you it is more of a croak. She must have been the identical twin sister of a toad in the *other* life. I am one of those people who believe in some kind of reincarnation: that a person has lived as some kind of creature before. Well, this particular creature must have belonged to either the reptile or viper family. Or she was a maggot. Feeding on rot.

'Madam, are you aware that this thing could find its way into the papers?'

The voice of the manager brings me back to the present. He has a point; gossip has been institutionalised in these parts.

'I don't care if it appears in "Have you Heard?",' I retort. I am referring to the gossip column of the leading daily around these parts. I would of course, deny it without a tinge of guilt if it appeared there.

'You wouldn't care? Am I hearing you right?' The manager is incredulous.

'I don't care a hoot. Like our people say, *owajwire tatiina mpango* if a woman takes off her clothes she does not fear the size of her partner's penis.'

So why would I not deny whatever the gossip columns allege? After all almost every politician says he has been misquoted. He says this then when he sees it in print he is shocked and denies it, saying he was misquoted.

But still our press leaves a lot to be desired.

However clear and categorical government officials get, the media somehow manages to get it wrong so often you get the impression they are always striving to get the messages the other way round. Usually it is the more sensational and controversial version, one that sends the public abuzz for weeks on end.

Recently, as the Kampala mayoral race hotted up, the President of the country who has gotten involved in this election mentions that whenever he looks at the *garbage* lying uncollected in the city he gets nauseated. We all hear him clearly and get it all on tape. But somehow the journalists *decide* they heard something different.

They quote the President as saying he feels like throwing up whenever he catches sight of the *Mayor*!

Another minister told me that whenever he says this shirt is *blue*, the media will confidently report that he said it was *red*! In many cases, what starts off as a *shirt* ends up as a *sheet*!

Then President Bill Clinton once said that if one day he miraculously walked on water like Jesus did, the independent media would not report that he walked on water. The screaming headlines would be:

'Bill Clinton cannot swim!'

It is also true that some government officials are press shy. These are the clock-like type, quietly busy, keeping time and content to produce no more sound than tick-tock. This kind feels a trifle shy talking to the press and will most probably refer them elsewhere for comment.

But usually the problem is with the media. In their efforts to get the sensational stuff and make it to the front page, journalists consistently end up getting the issues wrong, brewing storms in teacups and making mountains out of molehills.

To them, smelly socks in parliament is a bigger story than a $100 million grant to the country to build roads. The minister who used his shirt as a handkerchief makes bigger news than the project he opened at the occasion that will improve the lives of a thousand residents of that village. And the one who made a grammatical error in English will be a bigger story than the five million shillings he donated to a local dispensary.

* * *

'You have the ring? Madam, you have the *ring* but I have the *man*!' Her note of confident triumph sounds stronger than mine. All of a sudden, the ring feels heavy on my finger and I wish I could take it off and hurl it at Ishaka. And the way she keeps on sarcastically repeating *Madam* is enough to send me into an asylum. She has touched my raw nerve; she really has with that last knife thrust.

I cannot allow her to have the last word. I can't.

'You pig! (I have exhausted most of the animals, which I have been calling her. I think of resorting to amphibians, you know the toad and frog *thingys*. But I think I have already called her all of them. Including the ugly sounding mammals.) You can say what you bloody like. I don't care.' (Oh how I *do*! How I *do* care!) Then I put in a dramatic pause to get maximum effect.

'After all he spends three quarters of his time with me. He is with you just for a *few* hours in a month!'

There! I have the last shot. Floored you have I not, you hooded cobra? Shut you up forever.

Silence. Big one. I feel like shouting out in triumph. I have scored. World cup winner. *That* truth has definitely hurt her into dumbfoundedness. Before I can further wallow in my triumph, she comes in:

'It is called *quality* time, Madam. *Quality* time – those few hours we spend together. We'd rather spend a few precious hours together than having long, meaningless time. *Quality* not *quantity* time," she stresses. *Over* stresses.

I die. I am telling you. Death must be like this. It cannot be any worse.

I close my eyes and hold on to the wall for much needed support. I feel faint. There is this chill which has settled over my heart like...

There are things that are impossible to erase from one's memory. Words are things and I doubt whether I will ever wipe that *quality time* thing from my memory. It will remain etched there like an open sore.

'Please, Madam,' the Manager is quietly appealing to me.

Indeed I don't want to hear any more. She has had the last shot. As I start moving, *limping* away, I begin to wonder whether I should have subjected myself to this excruciating emotional pain.

I am like this queen whose husband used to bring lovers to a room in a different wing of the palace. The culture of the country permitted a king to bring lovers to the palace but to indulge in the illicit transaction in another section far from the prying eyes of the queen. This queen would know when the lovers arrived. She longed to know what exactly it was that her husband did with them. Maybe then, she thought, she would know the secret of why he was having sex with them. The eternal question of what do they have that I don't?

Unable to contain her curiosity, the queen drills a hole through thirty rooms into the king's chamber of sex. Through this hole, she watches her husband's sexual encounters with the myriad women. The more she watches, the more sickened she gets. She reaches a point where she cannot stand her husband. She feels a deep loathing for him. She decides to give up the watching but fails to because she is kind of *addicted* to it now in a sick kind of way. She is kind of hypnotised by it all – drawn to it like a rabbit to the lion that will devour it.

She loses appetite for food. She becomes emaciated, a shadow of her former self.

Until one day she can't take it any more and she bursts into the lust chamber, showers her husband and his lover with a hail of bullets. Then turns the revolver upon herself...

As I limp away then, I begin to doubt whether I have taken a wise decision by following Ishaka and his Manga. No. It definitely was a foolish decision. Suicidal. Next time, I will not listen to any so called friend giving me such a "tip". Though I am still not surc, is it better to know what is going on or to live in a fool's paradise? But according to Fina, in such cases ignorance is most certainly not bliss.

Oh she has scored, has the Manga fellow. I am hurt beyond repair.

'One last thing Liz. Let me give you advice, woman to woman.'

Of course I don't want to listen to her so-called advice. It is like a kite or hawk advising the chicken on how to hide. I don't want to hear but still the words come to me, clear. Too damn clear.

'Wanna know what is wrong with you so that you can put it right if you *can*? Liz, you have – had – an – engine – knock.'

She is spelling out every goddam word, taking her time.

'Engine *knock*. It needs a complete *over*haul, does your engine.'

And she bursts out in her trademark cackle.

'Let's go,' the Manager is earnestly hissing in my ear.

I don't need any further prompting to move. I have had enough.

As I move away, the sound of her cruel laughter, abruptly comes to an end. Then she starts crying. Curious, I turn back and so does the manager.

'Enough. Stop abusing her. She is human for God's sake. Suppose you were in her place. What would you feel for Christ's sake?'

'You still love her. You do.' She accuses him.

'Of course I care for her. Do not forget that she is my wife and the mother of my children.'

The Manager and I exchange surprised looks.

You just cannot believe what those words do for me. I feel elated, I feel the winner at the end of this soul bruising match. Oh how I wish men knew that it takes a few words to make the wife happy – in circumstances such as these. My cup is overflowing with happiness even though I know it is temporary. The crowning glory of the moment is to hear Manga break out in gasping sobs. Sorry baby. *So* sorry. I will buy you a huge handkerchief in which you can drown your tears. *Sniff, sniff.*

At least I have been *kinda* redeemed in front of the Manager and the hotel staff!

But my feel-good factor does not last long. When I reach home I throw myself dejectedly on the sofa. And this feeling of emptiness, of sadness envelopes me. For even though Ishaka told off Manga, he still stayed with her in the hotel. He did not walk out and he will not leave her. So where is my victory?

* * *

Ishaka, I also actually start wondering if you went to *her* because she has a better engine than mine although I don't know in what sense. This issue disturbs me so much that I start thinking of nothing else but how to better my performance in the bed department.

I admit I had long started taking Ishaka for granted, that since he said 'I do' and promised to be faithful, he would always be there for me and me only. How could I forget that many men only say those words strictly in honour of those present, not that they have any intention of keeping their word?

Do you recall, Ishaka, how one night I decide to play the proverbial tigress in bed? I have spent long sleepless nights trying to fathom what could have made you abandon me in favour of that wizard. Maybe she behaves like a *whore* in bed, every man's dream, I hear.

So I decide to imagine what she does and do the same.

As soon as I make up my mind, I go take a long bath. I scrub every part of my body more than ten times to make sure every cavity is clinically clean. I had already bought the sexiest perfume on the market – *Temptress.* The perfume smells exactly that.

Then I put on this tiny piece of thread that is supposed to pass for pants. I had actually felt terribly embarrassed while purchasing it and the shop assistant had given me this very queer look. But I ignored it and mumbled something incoherent about teenagers of these days who put on mere strings and call them panties. Then they embellish it by calling it a G-string.

I terribly miss my decent big ones, which teenage girls refer to in a derogative manner as the "Mothers Union" and swear that the type will never kiss their buttocks.

I then wrap myself up in a sexy, see-through *kanga.* The type that has these couples in wild romance, under the canopy of palm trees on sandy beaches. The very picture of paradise. Surely, Manga cannot be that imaginative. There is no way Ishaka will not be impressed. For sure he will turn up tonight. He has not yet started spending all his nights *there.*

It is approaching nine p.m. I will not eat any supper. Food has a way of bloating the stomach and having a full stomach before action commences – there is a way a full stomach kind of gets in the way. I will eat after the event. Let me instead swallow a tot of *waragi* brew for courage.

There he comes. My heart starts doing a marathon. Thump, thump, thump. My God! If it goes on like this, I will surely burst a blood vessel!

He is now opening the front door. And my thump, thump is getting louder.

The door is opening. I now must strike the pose of the irresistible woman. I throw one leg carelessly here and the other carelessly there. I lower my eyes, making them heavy in that bedroom eyes look.

'Hello darling! Welcome back. And tell you what, you are going to have me for dinner!' And I laugh in this low-tone sexy voice.

'What the hell do you think you are doing? Have you turned into a common cheap slut? Please leave that stupid act and put on some decent clothes. Remember you are a mother of two.' And he throws this very disgusted look at me as he storms into the bathroom. You remember the same look he threw at me when I confront him one night and ask him what has gone wrong with me. The way he keeps on repeating that I am a mother – as if mothers are not supposed to enjoy themselves.

I dash into one of the children's rooms and burst into tears. He mustn't see me crying for it would give him immense pleasure to know that he has hurt me.

Anyway, my plan has been a total flop. So much for my creativity.

Maybe the secret to Manga's success coup story lies in the way she dresses. I decide to do thorough research on her dress style. My mother says the way something is packaged makes a lot of difference to the beholder. The packaging either makes or unmakes you. Dress is a statement.

How then does Manga package herself?

Hmmm. I trail her on her way out with Ishaka. Like he affirmed, he has an appointment (with her) every day. (Puke, puke.)

Before they enter the car, I make sure I catch a good glimpse of her –rather of her dress. Or what passes as the dress.

The so-called skirt is something short of a big belt. The top covers only bits of her breasts. Three quarters of her tummy is all out on display. And, heavens above! She has pierced her belly button and there is a ring in it! Looking at that ring, I feel a gripping pain on my own belly button.

Oh Ishaka! How could you have preferred this woman who pierced her belly button to me?

Surely pierced navel is an indication that there is something terribly wrong with her morality! No decent woman goes around piercing her navel, or walks around, strutting her wares like she is available for whoever will.

I wouldn't be surprised if she has extended this piercing craze to *other* intimate parts of her body. I have heard of crazy women going as far as piercing their you know what.

'You know, Fina, at least Ishaka should have picked a decent woman. But to insult me with that thing that has pierced its navel!'

'Liz, it might be precisely because…'

I don't give her an opportunity to finish.

'Look, it is in the books. Based on research.'

'*What* is?'

'Listen to this: "...a parent should be very worried when her teenage daughter comes home with her eyebrow or navel pierced. A report released suggests a parent should be very worried because high school students with body piercings tend also to have smoked, used alcohol, had sex, skipped school and gotten into fights.

"The study, by Dr. Timothy Roberts of the University of Rochester in New York shows clear links between body piercings, other than the ears, and risky behaviour." There!'

Fina laughs.

'Now what's funny?'

'Look, the research you are quoting talks about teenagers not adults. So since Malaika…'

I glare at her. There is an unwritten law between us that we should never call her *that.*

'Sorry. Slip of the tongue.'

'Well, just make sure it does not get into the habit of slipping over that particular item.'

'Liz, I am trying to say two things if you will allow me to put in a word edgewise. One, that Mala – sorry, Manga – might have pierced her navel when already an adult in which case the issue of risky behaviour does not arise.'

'What are you trying to defend? Let me tell you; it does not matter when she damn did it. It just shows she is an e.g. of notorious, risky behaviour. A rebel of sorts.'

'Precisely. You have brought me to my second point. That one of her secrets, the very reason she managed to ensnare Ishaka is because she is a rebel of sorts, as you put it. It might be that she can do certain things which you can't; things that Ishaka finds attractive. Unconventional, untraditional things. Your un-rebel like behaviour has its own attraction for him, her rebellious nature completes his cycle. One appeals to his sense of decency, the other to his sense of adventure. That, Liz, balances his equation. Right?'

'Wrong. If any equation is balanced, it certainly is not Ishaka's. That guy has got the most unbalanced equation of all time.'

'You know, Liz, erase from your mind this thinking that he has insulted you by picking on a wretch like Manga. If he had picked a decent, beautiful woman, it still would have hurt you bad.'

Probably. Probably. There is this guy who announced "the first time I married beauty. Now I am marrying brains.'

I am marrying brains, my leg! Strictly for the cows. For a polygamist there will always be as many excuses as there are women. The first wife was okay, but she was not educated. Number two was educated, too educated and gave more time to her career than to me but number three had the best legs of them all. I had no plans to take on number three on full time basis; but she got pregnant during the affair and as a good African there was no way I would let my seed waste in the wilderness. As for number four, it is straightforward: she is bubbly, plump and delicious. Makes me feel several years younger.

Anyway, I was telling you about whether the way Manga dresses could have had something to do with her fatal attraction for Ishaka.

As she enters the car, the big belt that passes for a skirt goes higher, thereby exposing her pot-holed thighs and so on. As this happens, she tries to pull down the so-called skirt *mbu* to make it longer. For heaven's sake!

There is something detestable about a woman who does not have the *courage* to put on a mini-skirt or a multi-slitted skirt.

Yes indeed. It does take a certain amount of courage to dress this way. As for me, I confess to being a coward in this field, but I just think it is not right for me to dress that way. It's not that I condemn women who do so, especially when they are still young. Young like in below forty. I mean I like seeing young women in their miniskirts, giving us a sample of what the creator gave them, as we the judges award marks accordingly.

It is a mark of freedom, this mini-skirt thing, especially in Third World countries. The more the freedom the shorter the hem gets. In a dictatorship, women's rights are infringed upon, including denying them the right of freedom of dress. There was a megalomaniac of a president here some years ago who banned women from donning short skirts, something that introduced the era of the maxi-dress, a long, floor-sweeping affair that was quickly thrown out the moment the mental case (MC) was outgunned and overthrown.

My biggest problem for now, though, is that many women cannot stand up to defend their garb.

To begin with, she puts on this micro-mini to show off her good figure. Then when she is in the full glare of the crowd, she panics. She then embarks on the impossible task of trying to pull down the skirt in an attempt to make it longer. As if it is made of plastic, for Christ's sake!

It is bad enough to dress indecently especially when one is past a certain age. But it is worse when one does not have the courage to own up to one's manner of dressing.

* * *

We arrive at Kololo airstrip. Former airstrip really, turned parade ground. The place has been so built up, you'd never land even a tiny Cessna on it. But we still insist on calling it an airstrip. A kind of defiance against reality.

The Mitsubishi Pajero – an elaborate turbo and intercooler affair – stops. Two policemen appear as if from the air, on both sides of the machine and open the doors for us.

The master of ceremonies – a fellow who is apparently disblessed with the social graces of a pig, as he keeps grunting into the microphone from time to time – announces our arrival with such airs you'd think we are such close friends.

'And now, ladiiiiieeees aaaaand gentlemeeeenn, Mr...and...Mrs...Ishaka!'

I smile generously. This is a moment every lady enjoys; basking in the limelight alongside her husband at such a high profile occasion, especially one being captured live on national radio and television. More so when you know the likes of Manga are watching.

Ishaka touches my elbow, like a proud cock showing off its favourite hen, and we march towards the podium to take our seats.

Fina, here as chairperson of the Women's Movement, looks as though she is about to throw up. She glares at me, a deep, piercing look that penetrates my pupils, sears my heart and, for a moment, troubles my conscience. She knows that this is no more than a show and neither of us has their heart in it.

I quickly look away and spot Mr. and Mrs. Gooba, smiling for the cameras. Gooba recently married his wife's sister in a customary ceremony that for sometime had been the talking point of the community. Quite a few people voiced their protests, silently at first then vehemently later. The wife too protested seriously at what she deemed a gross injustice, having her younger sister as a co-wife.

But the parents settled the matter when they said they saw nothing wrong with the matter. As long as Gooba brought along the right brideprice, there was no problem. Besides, they pointed out to the elder sister, she would find it easier to deal with her own sister than with some unknown foreign woman. And, God forbid, if one of them died before the other, the surviving sister would look after her sister's children without any problem. There would be no repeat tales of stepmothers burning their step-kids or sending them to bed hungry, or something like that. And moreover, the old man said with an air of finality about the matter, it would be less strenuous dealing with one son-in-law than with two. One was burden enough, he said, before burrowing into his newspaper once again, to indicate that his words were finished.

Two rows behind the Gooba's, my eyes chance upon Dr. Tendo and his wife. The doctor, in his mid-forties and with a reputation for never doing a shoddy job; is a man everybody likes and respects. He is friendly and outgoing; a lover of people whom the people are only too happy to love back.

His wife is a woman everybody likes to hate for the simple reason that she is an accomplished snob, always talking about herself and her various giftings (which only she can see). To round it off, she has jumped into quite a few beds around town. After thinking seriously about the welfare of his kids and their possible discomfort should a step-mom step into the picture, the doctor apparently decides she can keep around. She is here today for purely official reasons; as an escort, unworthy though she be.

On the extreme right I see Hon. and Mrs. Fundi. Fundi who is one of the most senior parliamentarians, having been in at least four of Uganda's different parliaments, is eighty plus and looks it.

He has just a few teeth left and spends most of his time staring ahead into space and chewing his toothless gums in the process. His cheeks are deeply sunken and could hold an orange each without too much trouble. Try as he might to walk upright, the stoop is unmistakable and seems to be growing into a hunchback with each passing day. The hair, probably tired of being grey, is now turning into some other colour that the English language is yet to find appropriate vocabulary for.

But these not-too-flowery attributes have not stopped him from getting himself a succulent peach as second wife. She is only 26; a year younger than his first granddaughter.

Fundi's first wife, a gracious and beautiful woman has actually been through six decades. Fundi said she had become too old for him and he wanted some young pretty thing to rejuvenate his sexual appetites that many people said were legendary.

As everyone else (apart from bwana Fundi) knows, the young thing gets her bang from some young man of her own age group. The two children she has with Fundi look not too unlike the young man, whose excellent physique would promptly earn him a job as fitness instructor in any gym anywhere on earth.

A few big mouths have pointed out that while all Fundi's children resemble him in one way or another; these two have taken an unexplainable exception to this basic rule.

But Fundi who is also getting hard of hearing over time, is too busy chewing his toothless gums to hear any of this gossip.

On the extreme end I can see Bob the executive director of the leading beer company. He is in the company of his bitchy wife Anne; a nice-looking wench who is as beautiful as she is terrible to be around. You wonder how in the world such a fantastic man ended up with a witch like Anne. I think it is true after all, that opposites attract! Everybody knows Bob as a good chap – always in a good mood, with a kind word for everybody. He drinks, yes, but he is not a drunkard. But that Anne of his! She is always at him; in fact, all over him, accusing him of being a drunkard par excellence. Even after he's just sipped a glass of wine, she tells him not to 'come near me with all those alcohol fumes'. She behaves like she is the identical twin sister of the blessed virgin. Unlike her compatriot nearby, she does not jump into every bed, okay; but she is so cold, the room freezes when she walks in. And worse, she just never allows the poor Bob an inch of space to himself.

She is always all over him; tying him to herself and locking the whole world out. You'd think something (or someone) is itching to snatch or kill Bob the moment she looks the other way. For heavens sake, can't she see that she is suffocating him? Men like their space – plenty of it by the way; but Anne does not afford Bob any such liberties. She is always at him: 'Make sure you are home by 6.00 o'clock because dinner is at 7.00 o'clock and we must have it together.'

'You must take me to the islands this weekend. And don't you think of bringing your funny friends along...this is an out for two.' If Bob ever gets wife number two, no one will ask him what he is up to. They will only cock their heads and ask him what took him so long.

Next to Bob I can see Ndugu and his wife, Lynn. Ndugu – a well-bearded, deep-voiced and cool-headed fellow – also enjoys the enviable distinction of having, not only a pretty wife who is good and Godly, but also a very happy marriage. He is one of a select few high profile politicians whose cupboards are completely skeleton-free. If it is true that marriages are made in heaven, this one truly was.

CHAPTER FIVE

MAKE HER YOUR FRIEND

Today, I am not going to the office. I am totally fixed up. Entirely drained of all the positive emotions in a human being. I drag myself from bed, and to the bathroom. That's one other place I find refuge. I fill the bathtub with warm water, and my favourite foam bath. It's a beautiful sky blue liquid. I immerse myself in the water, and almost feel a sensual thrill as the water caresses my tired body.

The bath. Oh yes, it sure soothes me. Sometimes on a weekend, I can spend two solid hours in the bathtub. I swear.

They say a woman's work is never done. But one would also argue that a woman's bath is never complete. There are always a few things to tidy up. Some more soap here, a scrub there and a few more drops of water to complete the task. And just as you think you are probably done you discover there is a little more work to be done to the areas down south. Areas that you can never take chances with, lest the son of Adam find you a little too bushy for his liking. So out pops the shaver – don't we all carry a sharp and uncompromising pair of shavers in our little tool-boxes that we respectfully call handbags? She is no woman that hath no tool-box, I always say. That is the centre of our being, because it is the sustenance of our beauty. Any small mistake and all your hard work in the morning is undone. Sometimes I think that if we daughters of Eve were as vigilant at academics as we are at our appearance, we'd rule the world. With the kind of diligence we put into our aesthetics, nothing could beat us if we applied the same to the one area where the destiny of nations is determined.

I get out and check my watch: I was in the water for more than an hour. Talking to God. Though in between images of you-know-who keep flashing across. Uninvited, unwelcome images of the horned viper: Lucifer's beloved sister, Manga.

I go to the wardrobe, and get one of my *bitenge* which has lost colour. I should have given it away. I sigh, and put it on, and drag myself to the living room. The H.G. has already put my breakfast on the table: a platter of fruits, mixed juice, millet porridge and tea. I love millet: it's not only because of its nutritional value. I just love it.

Sometimes I am the typical African woman who eats something because it is nice; not because the doctors – or some self-appointed connoisseurs of nutrition – say so. In Africa it is the eye that decides whether or not the food is okay for the stomach. If it pleases the eye, down it goes. If it does not, forget the crap – never mind what the doctors say. We are not pigs to eat something that has no taste, just because some bookworm says it is good for the body. If the eye says yes, the mouth will have no objection and the stomach will sing from the same song sheet.

But unfortunately, most of the young generation abhors millet. These are the dot com children; a product of the computer era where everything is press-button or mouse-click. On several occasions when I have tried to make the children eat it, they have turned up their noses with the grace that a he-goat would envy, and said the stuff looks like soil! I cannot blame them too much (too moch, according to some Nigerian friends of mine), if I go back to my if-it-pleases-the-eye theory.

But last Christmas made them have a change of attitude. One of their cousins who lived in the States for years comes back home.

As usual, there is millet at dinner. My children make their usual it-looks-like-soil comment about it. Their cousin, however, has a different view: "Why, this looks like chocolate to me!" He declares, and commences to do justice to the millet bread with the passion of a duck showing what peas are for.

Mesmerised, my children try it tentatively, quickly make history of the millet and even ask for more! From then on, millet in the house achieves a 'highly endangered' status. Wonders never cease. And what does it? Nothing more wondrous than the chocolate look. That also improves my if-the-eyes-like-it theory considerably: I add a footnote to the effect that how the eyes see it is usually determined by how the mind views it. My goodness, I am sounding a philosopher already! And for good measure, I am feeling really intelligent, I can assure you. If I had lived in the times of the chaps like Socrates, I would be topping their Christmas card and coffee invitation lists, in their vain attempt to tap my wisdom.

I try to take the porridge which I relish so much but somehow it refuses to go down and, eventually, I throw myself on the sofa and stare into space.

After an eternity, I realise with shock that Fina is seated right by my side!

'My God, Fina, I did not see you coming in! Have you transformed into somebody from outer space, a kind of invisible woman?'

'Liz, I have been here close to two hours!'

'Impossible! Unless you want to say I have been in a coma, for Christ's sake!'

'You have said it; your words, not mine. I found you seated the way you are. Eyes wide open; staring at something only you could see. So intensely I got scared shitless.'

I wince a bit in mock shock at the language; then silence for a few minutes. Mock shock I say, because I have become the Queen of 'dirty language', more appropriately called 'four-letter words' in the contemporary version of the Queen's tongue. I acquired the crown when this thing of not being able to stand the Manga situation got into my head, so says Fina.

'I'm sorry, Fina.'

We both sigh, like two tired sows after a round each of bad sex.

'Anyway how are you Fina?'

'Fine. There is no need for me to ask you the same question because the answer is clearly etched on your face.'

'Oh no. I am fine, Fina. Very fine.'

'I can see it. You are damn fine. Oh, I can see it, Liz. In the deep circles under your eyes. In your eyes that are intensely focused on something, and yet on nothing. Yes. Your 'fine' is reflected in your zombie-like walk. In your somnambulistic walk – you know the sleepwalker. Yes, even in your drastic loss of weight. You are so fine you have made a wonderful figure because I can practically hear your bones rattling like a locomotive that is overdue for the next service. Come to think of it, you would comfortably win the prize for poor locomotion at the next beauty contest of this street junction.

'Your collarbones standing out like curved reeds around a freshly decorated Masai warrior's neck proclaim your state of 'fine'. Oh yes, Liz, you *are* fine.' She pauses. 'Come, Liz.'

Fina gets hold of my hand. I get up and she leads me to my bedroom. I stumble along like a faithful zombie that fully appreciates that asking questions is simply not in its nature.

She stops in front of the full-length mirror. 'Liz, look at that shattered visage in the mirror. That thing there is not you. Look at it again – perfect account of a scarecrow. Have you seen those starving Africans that CNN likes to parade? CNN seems to have a penchant for parading horror stories of Africans. Of children with oozing mucus and thousands of flies zooming about them? Children, either in advanced stages of starvation, or with bellies extended as if in the final month of pregnancy?

'In your state now, you would be a first class candidate for CNN's grizzly gory series: the embattled African housewife, or something along those lines.'

She sighs, and leads me to sit on the double bed – I look down and start counting my fingers.

'I have come so that you take a decision. You cannot remain the perfect victim for the rest of your life. Life is too short to be wasted just like that. You must take a decision.' She pauses. Then resumes. 'Liz, there is so much hatred and venom in your heart against Manga. Hatred is an acid that sooner destroys the carrier than the object it is meant to decimate. As some wise person put it, the grudge is now *holding you.* You are not the *one holding it!* You must take a decision.'

'On what?' I ask alert but wearily.

'On your life – I mean your existence. Like I have said before, you are merely existing. Not living. Let me tell you,' she adds in a soft voice, 'even if Ishaka wanted to leave the other woman, and have you once again as his only one, he wouldn't. For you look like some glaze-eyed, crooked-beaked, flat-bottomed and neck-twisted species of a duck.

'And that is the mistake women in your situation make. When a man gets another woman you give up on yourself. What you ought to do instead is try and look your best: go to the gym, dress well, be smart...'

I keep quiet - there is no more defence in me.

'So you have to take a decision pretty soon.'

'Am still waiting to hear what decision I should take?'

'Liz, in order for you to live again, I have come to present to you four options. One: Make yourself human again and get a man friend.'

I laugh.

'This is no laughing matter.'

'Fina, it is a cruel joke. Once bitten by a snake, you will flee at the sight of a lizard.'

'Liz, it is not as if this friend is going to marry you. He will just help you believe in yourself again and restore your self-confidence and self- esteem.'

'Please, Fina, do not repeat those things in psychology books. Anyway, I cannot go with a man unless I am in love with him.'

'You give him a chance and love will come.'

'For me it's the other way round. Love has to come before the chance and I believe by chance you mean sex.'

She nods in the affirmative.

'Anyway Liz, you don't have to find an answer now. Just think about it. Why should you waste away unloved while Ishaka is getting all the love he wants from his Manga?'

Silence reigns.

'That was plan A. Now we move on to plan B.'

'Yes?'

'Plan B is: befriend your co-wife. Make Manga your friend and the hurt will slowly melt away.'

She has touched a raw nerve, she really has.

'Fina, you are totally out of your mind. Befriend that fiend? My arch-enemy? Please. Or on reflection, maybe Manga has wormed her way into your heart, and sent you here as bait. So that she pretends to be my friend, get me close to her and finish me off!'

'Don't be silly. It has worked for some women. I mean, when they befriend their co-wife. Then the other woman ceases to be special to the man. She becomes like the official wife. The magic she holds for the man disappears. She becomes ordinary. Yes, it has worked for some women. In actual fact, Liz, there are cases of women who have urged their husbands to marry a girlfriend. 'Bring her home so that she also cooks', such women tell their husbands. The idea being that if this girlfriend becomes a wife, then the magic she used to hold for the man vanishes.'

'Well I am not some *other* women. There is no way I can be a friend with that she-goat. First, I would be the worst hypocrite because I know trying to make her my friend would not come from my heart. Second, I'd rather try to get water from a stone. Fina, if you have come to give me that bullshit, please get out of my house.'

'Okay, okay. Plan B has aborted. It's a stillbirth. So we move to C,' she says in this very strong voice.

'This is Plan C: get saved.'

I relapse into silence and confer with my thought apparatus.

I am not a born-again Christian. Somebody said he just cannot understand how one can be born again. That it is totally incomprehensible for one to be able to go back to his mother's womb and come out again. But I know it is true, it is possible to be born again. Trouble is, I also know I cannot make the grade.

I have too many human failings to make it. Little failings here and there that add up to a whole catalogue of failure. Just the kind of thing I imagine the Almighty would not be wont to put up with.

One thing though is: I do not set out to intentionally hurt people, but that's not the only criteria to qualify one as a born-again Christian.

The other reason I do not want to declare that I am born-again is that people will say I did it out of frustration. I hate it when people say that kind of stuff. Pisses me off, it really does.

Notwithstanding, my friend Fina's view that it is okay to get saved out of frustration because Jesus sent out an invitation to all those 'who labour and are heavy laden and I will give you rest'.

I truly believe in God and know that everything else is sinking sand. He has performed many miracles in my life. And as I despair over my shattered marriage, I know that it is only a question of time before He sorts it out.

I know He will because even as I fall into depths of despair, I can visualise Jesus' gentle loving, caring face smiling down at me and saying, 'The battle won't be long, girl. The pain will go away, and you will begin to live again.'

'Thank you Jesus,' I whisper to Him as I mentally repeat that timeless assurance that the good old Apostle Paul gave the Romans: 'If You be for us, who can be against us?'

But again I have some apprehension about becoming born again: I will have put myself in the dock. I will have lost my inherent right to be wrong, my God-given prerogative to make a mistake. At the slightest gaffe they will exclaim, 'What! How can you, a whole born-again Christian, do such a thing?' Everything you do becomes public debate; you are judged as though you are an angel, not a human. If you walk with a bit of a swagger, then you are trying to attract the opposite sex! If your skirt is above your knees, 'Look at her; who is she trying to hook?' They will ask.

If you sip a bit of beer, that is the ultimate: 'Look what a hypocrite we have here.' If you go to a party and hit the dance floor and shake your bones, you have failed the test. Will I make the grade? But then I wonder. What is the difference between some of this 'evil' dancing and that which we see in many Pentecostal churches these days, I ask you?

There is this young, smashing widow in Village Eleven, nicknamed 'Sprite', thanks to being so cute. She simply sparkles. She *is* born-again but many of the idle minds around here say that is impossible. These folks already have their minds made up about her promiscuity and all they are looking for is a small fact to prove their point. After she has smiled at three men along the street the harm is more than done.

'We told you so!' They bleat, jumping up and down in triumph like a rabbit that has just unwrapped a parcel of carrots.

The other reason I don't want to declare that I am born-again is the behaviour of some of the so-called born-agains. It just pisses me off. There they are shouting that if you are not born-again, you will perish in hell or something like that. Then you find they are having an affair with somebody secretly; or they are so cruel to the dependent relatives they are staying with.

I know some people who thrive on sin in their younger and better days. These barons of 'social' sin leave no skirt untouched and no bra innocent. Empty bottles, gourds and calabashes lie in their wake; and the chimneys in the neighbourhood are no match for their nostrils when it comes to letting the smoke out. They are as faithful with government coffers just as much as *bwana* Fox was when in charge of the chicken pen. Their female counterparts go on a sampling spree; carrying every male frame as though they have a duty to do so. When they go to dance they shake their buttocks in ways last seen in Sodom and Gomorrah. They break up countless homes and marriages as they lure all the paterfamilias to their lairs. From time to time, housewives all over the place get heart attacks as strange women dump kids on the doorstep. There is no need to ask whose kids they are; nature conspires to make sure the little creatures are exact miniature versions of the man of the house.

I am talking about the gurus of waywardness who sin as though they are the ones who invented sin. When they are too old to sin any more they become born again. *Then* they start condemning sinners and frowning upon them – even though the people they condemn haven't sinned even half as much as the pontificators did. They call them drunkards, thieves and adulterers and condemn them to hell.

Another fellow wears a cross on his lapel and carries a huge edition of the King James Version of the Bible. When it comes to interview time he cheats for his relatives. All this after claiming (and creating a class) that they are the ones who are holy and everybody else is a sinner. My view of being saved is that it is much more than claiming to be; it is about purity of the life you lead, the way you conduct yourself and the way you treat other people.

Like I told you I have a personal relationship with God and I'm always praying, but most of my prayers are never answered – at least not the way I want and expect them to be. This issue disturbs me so much that I go to my pastor and put it to him. Then he tells me a little story.

There was this man who welcomes Jesus to his house. Happy and excited at having the King of Kings, he gives him one of six rooms in the house. Jesus too is happy and takes up residence immediately. A fortnight later, robbers break in, beat up the man and take whatever they want.

Distressed, the man confronts Jesus bitterly. 'Master, how could you do this to me? How could you allow these thugs to rob me clean, when you were here all the while?'

Jesus was the perfect gentleman. 'I am sorry, but I am only a guest here and have authority over just one room,' the Lord explained. 'There is no way I would overstep my authority.'

The man saw the point and gave Jesus one more room, to make it two.

Shortly, the robbers return. Another beating, more cargo ferried off.

He confronts Jesus again. Same complaint. Same explanation: 'I had just two rooms; it would be ungentlemanly to overstep my authority. This is your house, not mine. It would be rude to usurp your authority.'

A little wiser, the man gives Jesus another room, making him 50 percent shareholder.

The robbers return, enjoy themselves immensely and Jesus does absolutely nothing. Same complaint, same answer.

Now truly wise, the man hands over the house keys to Jesus, giving him full authority over his estate.

Presently, the robbers return, hoping for another exciting, robbing spree. But a surprise far from pleasant, awaits them. They find the owner of the premises – none other than the Lord Himself – outside the door, waiting for them. They never know what strikes them and within moments they are past tense.

'One needs to fully surrender to the Lord before the Lord can take control of his life,' explains the pastor. 'If He is not Lord of all in your life, then He is not Lord at all.'

I am not sure I understand him too nice, so he continues.

'There are blessings that God gives to us inspite of our unfaithfulness. Those are the general blessings which He gives to us by covenant; like sunshine and rain, day and night. But there are also those special blessings – those that affect our specific destiny and concern God's perfect plan for us – which we can only enjoy if we are fully surrendered.'

I sigh heavily…

'Here is plan D: You walk.'

Fina's firm statement wakes up Alice from her wonderland.

'Walk? What do you mean walk? I have not been running a marathon, have I? You want me to become a streetwalker? Fina, please get serious.'

'I have never been more serious in my life. I mean walk as in walking out of the marriage, period.'

In the heavy silence that follows you could hear the proverbial pin drop. Fina's eyes interlock with mine until mine drop.

'Yes, Liz, walk. It's the only alternative. For look, you yourself have told me that you are not even having sex with Ishaka. For how long will he accept your refusal? So you either accept to stay in this polygamous marriage, and carry out the most essential part – sex – or you walk!'

The silence reigns heavy. Even a graveyard gets louder than this, surely.

The tick-tock of the clock becomes pronounced. The yelping of Bruce the teenage dog becomes louder, like he has seen the bitch he craves. The cooing of the dove nesting in the eucalyptus tree in the compound intensifies. And the whistle of my happy-go-lucky *shamba* boy now sounds sharper as he continues with his work.

'See you later, Liz. It's not easy,' she says softly. 'But as I told you before, impossible situations demand a clean cut and in order to make an omelette, you have to break an egg before you can get the yolk,' says Fina as she slowly walks out.

'Fina. A minute.'

She pauses at the door.

'I am not walking. Marriages are made in heaven,' I say quietly.

'That is bull. So is thunder and lightening. They too are made in heaven,' she says contemptuously as she bangs the door after her.

CHAPTER SIX

CROSSROADS: THE ROAD NOT TAKEN

I've just been reading one of my favourite poems. (It's full of sighs.) I sigh, too. That's what my life has become... one long sigh. But that's a sure sign of a victim, as Fina said. I must put a stop to this sighing business; it is not the stuff victors are made of.

Fina has sent my mind on a whirlwind of thought. Indeed! I agree with her that I must make a decision. It is also true that ever since Ishaka got Manga, I have put an embargo on sex with him. It happened mentally. Whenever he approaches me for sex, I literally freeze. I become frigid because what cuts across my mind is him having sex with Manga, and I can't take it. I will not lie down and watch him have his fill and then scream Manga's name when he reaches the mountain top. I won't have him take me in his arms in the dead of night and whisper 'I love you more than I ever loved any other woman' to my ears.

I just cannot. Intimacy flew out of the window.

Even on the rare occasions that we have had a meal – on the bedroom table (once or twice, I think, when I felt I needed something to quicken the body a little), it has been a quick-quick affair. Just a few fingers of *matooke* dumped in water, salt thrown all over and boiled for a few minutes and then wolfed down with such speed you'd think we are soldiers at the front line, getting the food over with so we can resume more important business. Not the more traditional *matooke* that is thoughtfully and elaborately prepared, mashed skilfully, left to steam on the fire for some time then slowly unwrapped and gracefully eaten with relish, savouring every swallow and praising the cook endlessly.

Polygamy just makes it difficult for intimacy to be sustained between husband and wife. Sex is relegated from the ultimate expression of love to a mere duty, especially for the estranged wife.

A friend – a first wife herself – caught in such a situation decides to stay in the marriage. She says when the husband demands for sex, she dutifully presents her body. She is totally detached from the act. In her own words, the man might as well be having sex with a piece of wood. Or like in some frigid woman where, while enduring sex, the woman asks for fish and chips.

Nothing these days like the good old-fashioned sex we were used to, I carrying on a running commentary while my dear Ishaka did all the needful. Now on the very few occasions when Ishaka wants to have sex with me, he shoves his big toe towards my foot. Then presses the damn toe against my foot. Actually it is more like his stupid toe kind of kicks against my foot. Very loving way of asking for it. In response, I aim a deadly blow at the goddam toe.

As I ponder on my next move, I wonder why the traditional African woman accepted polygamy. I ask around. Maybe I did not have to do so much research in order to find out the truth.

Marriage in Africa had really nothing to do with love. The traditional African man never married for "love" – it was out of necessity. Free labour for his farm(s); and complaint or rebellion was unimaginable.

The first wife was always respected. More highly respected by the husband than all the other wives. But modern day polygamy is built on totally different premises. The other woman comes as a competitor, to snatch love from the official wife for herself. Her life is focused on nothing else but to show the official wife that the man loves her better. She will do anything to hurt the official wife; maybe not physically, but anything that will torture the her rival's spirits real good.

Like this woman Carol who comes in as number two. She quickly starts on making life miserable for Nita the number one. Within a short time the husband takes Carol to the Carribeans on holiday. Carol makes sure they take elaborate and erotic photographs that capture the passionate moments of the holiday and then posts the photographs to Nita 'with love'. In one picture the couple are lying naked on the sand under a palm tree, kissing passionately. In another, Carol is pouring some drink or other - from her mouth - into the bastard's mouth, like a bird feeding her young. Nita flips through just three or four pictures before blacking out completely for a few days, waking up to find herself in hospital..

If the man is Uncle IMF – when fate has smiled at his purse – the other woman will demand that he buys her the latest car. She makes sure the first wife comes to know of it. Better still, the wife must see her driving this fantastic car. Must be a four-wheel affair, complete with all the luxuries that go with it – especially the intercooler and turbo facilities. With the love we have for Japanese cars, this must be a Pajero, Surf or Prado or something as good.

It is not unusual for one to get what they think is a strange problem that can only originate from outer space and they confide their fears in a friend, only to find that the friend has exactly the same problem.

That is precisely what happened the other day. Some friend of mine – an official wife herself – feels good when her husband buys her a Toyota Carina, a small albeit cheap affair that is a handy shopping basket. But the feel-good factor lasts a few months and ends when she meets her co-wife in the parking lot of their husband's working place.

She has no interest in the huge Landcruiser Prado that is reversing out of the parking lot until it seems the driver's face is vaguely familiar. As, with great difficulty, she maneuvers the Carina in a small space just beside the posh and sparkling mass of metal, she chances to look up at the driver of the huge machine that moves with the smoothness of raw egg down the gullet, towering high above her and ridiculously dwarfing the little noisy Carina in a typical David-Goliath scenario.

From her lofty perch, the driver of the Prado flashes a toothless grin (courtesy of a bar brawl not too long ago with her husband) and waves cheekily. That is when my friend realises it is her co-wife.

But it is too late to return the grin or offer a jeer in return, because with one step on the gas, the priceless machine shoots out of the gate with the sleekness of a gazelle, leaving the Carina occupant in distress as she compares the fortunes of the two drivers and coming up with no encouraging results on her part.

But the real distress is yet to come.

A fortnight later, the whole village learns – thanks to her rival's impeccable communication skills – that the *Bwana Mkubwa* (big man) is taking Number Two on a shopping spree to London. For some reason the departure is upgraded from a private issue to a public concern; a huge chunk of the village is present to witness the rich man afford his second wife – Madam Prado as she likes to be called – a favour the first one (Madam Carina as the neighbours call her to distinguish between the two women) has not even seen in her dreams. As the British Airways Boeing 747 soars over the area, gaining height as it begins its long haul to the land of the Queen where it is said (in awe around here) that even little children speak English, Madam Carina looks up and her spirits sink.

For a fleeting moment she prays it will crash, but then realises that would leave her a widow and anyway, even those innocent passengers on board would never survive. Slowly she bows her head and asks God to forgive and deliver her from evil thoughts.

I have already stated that I am not one of those women who, when a third party enters the relationship, wishes that the man should die so that 'if I can't have him, neither should she.' Madam Carina is obviously of a similar persuasion as myself.

She is pure and simple, that woman who told King Solomon that she'd rather her nemesis took the child alive than have the kid chopped into two for each to take half. You can tell who the real mother is, and you can tell who the real wife is, even if the man has 20 of them.

In modern day polygamy your typical Number Two will make sure the man builds her a better house than Number One's. And it must be in a place where everybody sees it, points fingers of envy and says: 'Ah! Look at that gorgeous mansion. Ishaka built it for his second wife.'

In traditional polygamous marriages, the most beautiful house belonged to the official wife. It was known as the big house. The small house belonged to the second wife, a symbol that she was the lesser in status. With modern day polygamy it's the other way round.

The practice of having an official wife has been mutilated, murdered and buried by modern day polygamy and the last funeral rites held for it. May its soul rest in peace.

Indeed on one rare occasion when I happen upon Manga and boast that I am the official wife, she scoffs – and rightly so I think – that we are *both* official wives of Ishaka.

'What is on you that is not on me, your dead lizards notwithstanding?' She sneers.

I am suddenly short of words. I hobble away like a wounded dog.

In those bad old days those women were illiterate, had few options in life and didn't know better than to obey without question. They had no problem sharing a man.

What I don't understand, though, is why a graduate like Manga who knows her rights, and has the means to live independently if she so chooses, should agree to become a second – or third or fourth – wife. To be fair to Manga, she may be ugly but she definitely has presence. When she is around you cannot ignore her, try as you might.

Why should a woman like that agree to become one of several wells for some greedy pot or pan? Why should the pestle that pounds in many other mortars venture into her own as well? Or does she think "all is fair in love and war?" I sincerely would want to know why she would want to suffer this exploitation.

Fina whose intelligence gathering proficiency suggests she has a doctorate in espionage, offers her unsolicited, albeit fairly informed insight into why Manga agreed to become number two.

Unlike yours truly, who is usually in the dark about this and that, somehow Fina always manages to get all the juicy gossip around town. When she doesn't get it, it looks for her.

As is often the case with people of her mould, Fina is at the scene of crime one day at a party, when some woman asks Manga why she agreed to become wife number two.

Fina's eavesdropping ears twitch in eager anticipation.

'I did not know he was married,' Manga answers without hesitation, keeping a straight face.

'You didn't know he was married? I've heard that hogwash a thousand times over from every woman of your type. Try another lie.'

'In any case I fell in love with him and as you can see, he too fell in love with me. It was only sensible that we bring everything to its logical conclusion – marriage. Look, you have to grasp what you need. I needed love and I found the man to give it to me. So what the heck even if he is married.'

For some other second wives, the accomplished spy chief ventures, another woman stole her man and she took it upon herself to exact revenge against all women. So she makes it a point to steal another's man either once and for all or every so often, whenever the need arises.

Other women, my connoisseur volunteers will simply plead loneliness. In relationship jurisprudence this is the equivalent of pleading insanity to a murder charge. The basic reasoning that both judge and jury will readily appreciate is that a woman lonely for too long is not responsible for the consequences of her pursuits or the extremes her desire drives her to. Married or not, a man is a man and will supply much-needed male company.

And in any case, in those days gone by, customary marriages were what took place. The man courts his woman and pays dowry and takes her for his wife. After a few years, his shamba grows bigger. He must marry another...he goes through the same cycle.

To date, the Christian African polygamist is caught between the devil and the sea. He takes his first wife to church. In the presence of a full church, the couple take the marriage vows. This marriage is the voluntary union of one man and one woman for life to the *exclusion* of all others.

But the African man can still go through a customary ceremony of marriage! A man weds in church, then later falls in "love" with another woman and takes her through a customary marriage. On the other hand, a man who acquires his first wife through customary marriage, when he gets a second one he says 'Ah, I am going to wed you in church because I have never wedded'.

And therein lies the tragedy of our Christian societies. Most African have not completely embraced Christian values. Maybe there is something Christianity does not fully answer in an African – a missing link. They have one leg in Christianity and another in tradition. This is like worshipping two gods and one is bound to suffer at the expense of the other.

The missing link may also explain why many Christians turn to witchcraft! Come election time and you will see all but a few of the politicians trooping to the witchdoctors to procure victory. They will ask for a spell against their opponents and buy charms that will give them favour before the people. The witchdoctor, careful to appear at his best when it matters most, will dutifully dispense his charms – sometimes to two opponents at different times – and charge them punitively, reaping a huge profit in the process.

From there the same politicians will march into church with all piety and join the faithful in worship and ask the priest for a blessing.

If they truly believed, would they surely turn to such practices?

Society condones this double life. Why else would practising Christian parents hold a ceremony to give away their daughter to a man whom they know wedded in church?

Take Manga. Her parents know that Ishaka is properly married in church. He has not divorced and they know it. Forget about divorced; he has not even separated from his wife. However, they proceed to hold one of the most lavish give away ceremonies for her. Giving her to Ishaka. When my spy tells me what a great ceremony it was, I puke. I really do. Though at the end of the day, I find out that sometimes it is poverty that drives such parents to 'sell' their daughter to the highest bidder.

I would have forgiven Ishaka if he had made it clear right from the word go that he was marrying me under customary law, which recognises polygamy. But of course I would have refused to marry him, because I am not made of the stuff that accepts polygamy. He would have made his pick though and been free to contract other marriages. But to make a mockery of church weddings!

* * *

Fina has really done it. Every minute of my life, I am thinking of nothing else but the decision to take. I waver between staying and walking. I now fully agree with the Jews who say that life is like a bowl of sour cream. This Manga woman has certainly set me sipping it all day every day.

After a month of intense thinking, I reach a decision.

'Fina, I have decided to stay,' I tell her on the phone.

'Fine. That means you are accepting the situation. Therefore, from now onwards, stop fretting. Stop sulking. Stop having a pity party. Stop nagging Ishaka. You have accepted Manga as your co-wife and stop coming to me for a shoulder to cry on."

I keep quiet.

'Are you there, Liz?'

'Yes, I am still on the line.'

'You have taken an important step. Acceptance. Now get out and live. Learn how to live with it. It will, of course, take some time but since you are now resigned to your fate, it will be easier to handle.'

Resigned to my fate? Is that what it is?

'Yes, that is what it is.'

God, she has read my mind.

'So, Liz, you know what, since now you have accepted the situation, you can actually be friends with Manga.'

'What? You must be crazy!'

'No I am not. But since now you have accepted her as your co-wife, you might as well become friends. She comes to visit you, you go to visit her. Then he will start treating her as a wife, not a lover. You know a man cannot sleep without seeing his lover. So make her your friend.'

'Over my dead body,' I say between my teeth.

'Anyway, it will take time but since you have *accepted*...'

"Please do not repeat that word 'accepted' if you want us to remain friends," I say tersely.

I am getting fed up with that 'accepted' business. It is getting up to my neck.

'Hold fire, hold fire, Liz. Take it easy.'

'Fina, I don't expect that crap of 'take it *easy*' from you. Anyway, Fina, I am thinking deeply. I will call you later.'

Indeed I *am* thinking deeply.

'That means that you accept that polygamy is the normal and African thing to do,' Fina tells me.

'Fina. I thought we said not to use the word 'accept' ever again. I am not 'accepting' the polygamous situation. But I already have two children with Ishaka so, for me, it is easier to stay than to leave. I am not accepting it... I am just resigning myself to it.'

'Just accept her as your co-wife,' Fina ventures, trying to be of some help.

'Don't give me any of your co-wife bullshit,' I spit back.

God, how I hate the word 'co-wife'! It brings to mind stuff like co-education or co-curricular. In other words the situation is so normal, you are pretty comfortable existing alongside it. Other women shorten it to 'co'.

'Oh, I am going to see my *co*,' they whimper despicably. I feel this onrush of nausea. Pass me the sick bag!

There is one thing I must thank Ishaka for, though. Of course I will not thank him to his face. Believe you me, I am at least happy that he has made it known that he has another wife. I mean it. I mean I'm glad that he has made it public. Because look, many a married woman for a long time imagines she is the one and only wife. Until death strikes the man. Then she gets the shock of her life.

Like this cousin of mine, Lydia. She is happily married. Her husband never spends a night out unless he is on safari. He is so loving. The type that even goes to the kitchen just to be with the woman of his heart. When Lydia is cutting onions, he is doing the tomatoes. When she is washing the dishes, he is drying whatever she finishes.

He has a big photograph of her (framed in *gold*) on his office table, carries a miniature version of the same in his wallet, calls her twice or thrice a day while at the office and takes her out three times a week, never mind he is always busy. For this couple, everyone says, the honeymoon (some goon with coarse manners called it a 'horny moon') has never really ended. It still goes on and on. I don't like the sound of 'horny moon'. But when some neighbour of Lydia's tells me that Lydia and her husband attack each other like dogs even before the lights are out all round the neighbourhood, I agree that this is quite appropriately called a horny moon.

Even after more than a decade in marriage, this couple seem starved for each other. On one occasion the husband walks in and grabs Lydia, throws her on the bed, undresses her quickly and proceeds with business, oblivious to the fact that the curtains are not drawn and a neighbour is watching all the action live and free. As the couple quench their thirst, an observer would be forgiven for mistaking them for newly weds who have carried their virginity to the marriage bed and are trying to make up for all the time they lost, each sparing them for the other.

Lydia says he is probably one in a million, one of the few men that do not seem to have a contract of mounting every woman in town. Given the passion with which he attacks her whenever he comes home, it would not be intelligent analysis to say he is unfaithful to his wife.

Then the angel of death strikes him down in a grisly car accident. Lydia is devastated. Understandably, since he is the only man she had ever known and the only one blessed with the privilege of seeing her nakedness. The lucky old goat had enjoyed patent rights to this wonderful piece of nature!

The church is packed to capacity for the funeral service.

'Fellow mourners, I now call upon the widow, Lydia to come and lay her wreath.'

Lydia gets up with dignity and places her wreath on the coffin. As she sobs her way back to her seat, she comes face to face with a tall beautiful woman who – if she were not sobbing uncontrollably – looks a perfect reincarnation of the lean-figured and fine-legged Cleopatra.

The grief is unmistakable; no actress would do it this good. Just the kind of sobbing to inspire a great offertory and make the eulogists quickly add a few more footnotes to their prepared speeches.

'Oh Richard, Rich! How can you leave *me*? Why didn't God take me instead of you? I can't live without you. I *can't* !'

After a good albeit quick comparative look at the two women, one indiscreet observer remarks rather too loudly and above the sobs that this one looks the *real* widow. Her sobs have more grief in them and her tears certainly *look* more salty, he explains to nobody in particular.

Lydia's tears dry immediately. Who the hell is *this* woman? Everyone is in shock – it hadn't struck them that the sobbing rights at this function belonged to anybody *other* than Lydia. This woman who is calling Richard, Rich? It is only Lydia who calls him Rich!

To crown her *brilliant* performance, 'Cleopatra' faints. The perfect way to round off what has certainly been an excellent concert, except that she is not awake to make the customary bow as her audience all rise at once. No problem about the bow, as it turns out the audience is not rising to give what would have been an appropriate standing ovation. They are simply aghast at what has befallen their heroine.

'Who is *she*?' People whisper.

'Apparently old Rich had a *spare* tyre.' The indiscreet narrator is back to work and now he has an even more willing audience, already spellbound by his analysis and eager for more. 'And this simply serves to prove my theory that not all motorists get the typical *plain* and *unremarkable* spare tyres,' he adds without feeling, like a police officer giving details of a horrific accident while careful to remain distant from all emotions associated with such happenings.

Lydia is aghast. After a minute or so, she breaks into fresh wails. But this time everybody is sure it is *not* the dead man she is mourning. And the indiscreet narrator promptly observes that this round of wailing is sharper and more passionate than the previous one. Nobody doubts him.

'May I now invite the deceased's children to come and lay their wreaths,' the master of ceremonies continues, unfazed by the drama. The way things are happening (and his black suit, notwithstanding) he could as well be the announcer at an elephant circus (blue is the perfect colour for this kind of thing), calling for the smaller versions of the huge mammal to come and display their abilities.

Lydia has two children, a boy and a girl. They tearfully take their wreaths as they cry: 'Daddy! Daddy!'

But the wiser folks among the mourners look around for some other little people who must surely emerge from somewhere.

Their wisdom proves beyond question as the two kids are soon joined by *three* others – each a perfect photocopy, kind of *clones,* of the dead man – also laden with wreaths screaming: 'Daddy, why have you left us?'

This time, it is *Lydia* who faints.

Again, the indiscreet narrator points out that this faint has more life in it than the one of 'Cleopatra'. By now everyone is hanging on to this man's every word, as it is clear his analysis is impeccable.

Through a cloudy haze, Lydia buries her husband. 'Their' husband is more like it. Her woes do not end there.

Lydia is shocked that this mistress or whatever, whom she did not even know existed, is actually a wife and is treated as her equal before the law when it comes to inheritance! The woman actually takes a large share of the property to which Lydia contributed so much, if not *more* than Richard did.

For instance, at Lydia's give-away ceremony, when the family officially hands her over to the bridegroom, true to tradition, her family gifts the couple some cattle to start their new life with. Some five heads of cattle do the journey to the new home.

After 22 years of marriage, the couple has more than 100 heads of cattle, thanks to careful, elaborate and enterprising breeding.

When Richard dies (without making a will) the cattle are divided equally between the two sides of the family; and 'Cleopatra', who did not participate in making the dinner, is made to occupy a prominent place at the dinner table.

Lydia is incensed, arguing that the cattle were donated by her family and so her new rival (who it was now clear, has actually been around all the while) has surely no business getting part of it.

The official from the Administrator General's office will have none of this though. He mumbles that as far as he is concerned, all the property had been registered as belonging to the deceased. His work as an implementer of the law is simple: chop the property into two, as the law demands, so that each side of the family benefits in equal measure from the deceased's estate. The internal dynamics of how this property came into the family is a matter completely irrelevant in the law and is none of his business.

He then proceeds to divide the estate without another word in respect of Lydia's protestations.

Some four houses in the city that the couple built on Lydia's initiative and with more than half the money from her coffers are next on the list. They too are to be shared between the two women

This time however, Lydia dons a new mantle. It is relatively okay about the cows, she decides, although silently praying that lightening strikes the ones 'Cleopatra' has stolen. How can the viper take cows that came from my father?

Those can always be replaced at any time. The houses though, are a different kettle of fish.

Not only did she contribute most of the money; she also personally supervised their construction, making sure everything was done according to the initial plan and that the workers did not help themselves to the building materials, as they are wont to do in such circumstances.

Completing four houses had been no mean feat and had certainly drained the resources quite a bit. For a long time the couple had paid dearly for the investment, living on scraps till the times got better; only comforted by the knowledge that the houses were complete.

And now, the Hyena that had watched from a cowardly distance as the lions tussled with their prey was on the verge of sharing the spoils in equal measure.

'Over my dead body; law or no law,' Lydia declares, gathering her skirts and looking for the nearest handy weapon that might help ram some sense into this lawman's thick head.

'Do you know how much I sweated to get these houses built? Are you aware how much I sacrificed through it all? What are you saying, you cowardly son of a pig?'

The official, highly experienced in such matters, is well aware of just how dangerous an irate widow – first, robbed of a husband and now being robbed of hard-earned property - can be in such circumstances.

But the law is the law, he explains, adding that he did not write the law in the first place; he is only implementing it to the letter. Since these 'other' children also belonged to the deceased, the law provides that they too benefit from their father's estate. The question of the children's legitimacy was immaterial here, he points out, as he appends his signature at the bottom of the page, to show that the matter has been concluded.

Lydia bites her lips and clenches her small fists bitterly, as tears stream down her once beautiful face. She knows there is nothing much she can do about this now.

But she decides to form a pressure group to fight such injustice against widows in her position, so that at least her daughter should never go through such an ordeal.

In all this ordeal, Lydia feels a very strong hatred towards her late husband.

"I know it's no use hating a dead person; and that it is the ultimate in bad taste. But I hate you Richard. I hate you even in death, more than I loved you when you were alive. At least you should have let me know; for this betrayal is more than I can bear," she seethes as she throws *grass,* (dry grass at that) on his grave on the first anniversary of his death.

* * *

It is two months after that talk with Fina. I get up from this cosy single bed.

Eva is at the door looking like the Amazon.

'I want my Daddy,' she roars as she stomps her feet.

'Eva, Daddy is on safari.'

'That is what you said yesterday.'

'He will come tomorrow.'

'That is what you said yesterday!' She screams, her eyes glowing like hot charcoal.

'Eva, you are calling your mother a liar. Your Father will come – well one day.' I end on a lame note.

'No he won't. I want a teddy bear. NOW.'

That is how she gets to extract things from me. I don't blame her entirely; this is one trait that runs in the family.

'Alright. I will bring it.'

'Now. I don't like this house. Too small. We go back home. NOW.'

'Honey, this *is* home.'

'No it isn't! Home, the other big house with Daddy,' she screams as she angrily stomps her foot.

I sigh, like a cow whose calf has refused to suckle.

Eva is now a bundle of nerves. She throws tantrums. She screams every other minute. Not once, not twice, she throws objects at me. Cups, saucers. Anything she can lay her hands on. I have had to hide anything that looks lethal. For there is this day when she has been screaming that she wants her daddy. I tell her the usual 'he'll come tomorrow.'

'Don't give me that horse manure!' she screams.

'Eva!' I yell back, trying to put things under my control once again.

And before I know it she is holding this carving knife with an evil glitter in her eyes. The things movies do to our little ones! I lock away all knives after that, lest she plunges one into my tummy or – most probably – into my back as I am looking the other way, one of these days.

On one occasion I am busy cleaning the kitchen floor, fully bent and all attention focussed on my work, when something urges me to look behind. My eyes promptly grow egg-size at the sight of my own daughter holding a flower vase and preparing to smash her mom with it. I stumble aside just in time, as the vase whizzes past my head and crashes loudly onto the floor, pieces scattering in all directions.

The flower vase has been around for a few years now; but it had never occurred to me that it could be used for any purpose other than to hold flowers! At this rate I should probably hide the chairs and tables as well; you never know... .

I can't believe the profane language coming out of her! Reminds me of the little girl in that sick book *The Exorcist*. The girl who got possessed by a demon.

Indeed it is as if a demon has taken over Eva's entire being. She is restless. Has no appetite.

'I want Daddy to come and feed me. NOW!' She stomps, with the passion of a soccer hooligan whose team has just lost another game courtesy of a bad referee.

Everything must be done TODAY and NOW. Her father had spoilt her rotten. Whenever it was lunchtime, he'd come to feed her. She'd tell him: 'Daddy, take me to the tap, let the water flow and feed me.'

He'd proceed to do her bidding. Crazy. He'd actually get her, sit her next to the sink, open the tap and feed her. And she puts one hand under the tap and lets water flow over it! As her father feeds her.

Eva is my biggest problem now.

I did walk, you know. I sat and thought of accepting the situation, accepting Manga. And it proved impossible. Some women can stand it. I am not one of them. Let Manga have Ishaka to herself.

The second reason I had wanted to stay was what many people sneer at: for the sake of the children. I am not one to sneer in this regard.

But when Ishaka starts ignoring the children completely then I reason that well, even *that* reason has gone *kaput*.

Ishaka has no space for both children now. In the past, as I said, he used to enjoy fixing things around the house with Kirabo. It created a strong companionship feel between them. But that is all history now, because he has no time for the kids.

Kirabo who is 18 one day tells his father that his school basketball team is going to have a match with that of a nearby school. Naturally he wants his dad there as usual, to watch from the stands as he (Kirabo) dishes out a tough basketballing lesson to the opponents.

'Are you crazy?" His surprisingly irate dad asks. 'I have far better things to do than watch that stupid game of yours.'

The hurt look in Kirabo's eyes, the deflated pride visible all over his face and the shrunken shoulders as reality sinks in the young man's understanding will forever be in my memory.

As it turns out the "far better things" Ishaka had to do are simply that Manga's brother who is going overseas for further studies is having a congratulatory and send-off bash in his honour at some beach or other.

On another occasion, my Eva, who is used to being hugged and swung up and down by her dad; comes running to him when he returns home one fine evening.

'Daddy swing me,' she cries happily, expecting the usual answer.

She is not prepared for the refusal that follows.

'Don't be silly Eva,' he growls without another look at her. 'You are too big to be swung around. You are no longer a baby. Stop those bad manners you are picking from your mother and behave like your age.'

All of a sudden, within just a few months, Eva is too grown up to be swung by her dad. How is a six-year old supposed to know how to behave like her age?

The tears that gush from my daughter's eyes as she stands in shocked silence, in a long moment of complete incomprehension; pierce my heart deeply. I take Eva to her room, hold her gently in my arms and we both weep; silently but very bitterly.

Yet I know that inspite of the painful rejection, the children still love their dad.

Later on I share my pain with my grandma, telling her everything about Ishaka's complete aversion to his children.

'He no longer loves them,' I assure her. 'They are no more than fleas in his armpit, from his point of view; sheer footnotes in his life.'

I know grandma knows all there is to know about fleas, having eaten humble pie for most of her life. But I doubt she knows too much about footnotes. Anyway, I hope she gets the point somehow.

'Child,' grandma begins, looking me straight in the eye. 'That is no surprise. *Embabazi z'omwana ziruga aha kinyi kya nyina.*' There is no way a man will have affection for the children if he is not enjoying sexual intimacy with their mother.

Walking was not easy. I just get up one morning and decide not to stay another hour. Suddenly Liz, who has been adamant about not leaving, can't wait to be out the door. I pack my bags. There is this urge in me to leave a farewell note, the way the suicide chaps like to. But I hate those farewell sloppy notes lovers always leave behind after separation.

So I just leave. I tell Kirabo the truth, but tell Eva that we are going on vacation.

'Without Daddy?' She asks her face a mask of disappointment. A father is the whole and entire life for his daughter. She won't reason much – or any – beyond that.

'He will join us later,' I tell her.

'Well, it won't be much fun without him.'

'Don't worry. He will come and we shall have fun.'

She glares and puts her tongue out at me.

'Young lady, remember that I am your mother. And I most certainly won't brook this insolence, you young puppy. I would like you to know that I am your mother and there is nothing you can do about it since I do not have to seek re-election to this particular office!'

'Some mother. Mother who wants to leave Daddy,' she shouts with a sneer that would make demons wince.

I am the guilty party in her eyes. And as it is certain she cannot see sense in this condition, I hope to make her understand one day. Some day.

Kirabo is not amused either. He is in a perpetual sulk. He says he feels humiliated, saying his friends are laughing at him, after learning that his parents have split up. I tell him that this will pass soon, but he is not impressed. He remains completely inconsolable.

Moving away and starting life all over has not been easy. The day I pack my things and leave is like a bereavement. Like I have severed the better chunk of my life. When you have slept under the same blanket with somebody for more than twenty years, it's not easy to call it quits.

Funny I know, but from the day I leave, I keep on hoping that Ishaka will call.

'Liz, why the hell have you moved out on me? I miss you so much. Please come back.'

Like every woman whose relationship has ended, I long to hear that, even though this is the last thing I would admit to anybody, including myself. But he doesn't call. And I cease to expect his call.

But sometimes I get tempted and call his cellphone. Then as soon as he picks it and says the customary 'hello', my throat somehow runs dry and I get tongue-tied. He mutters angrily about idiots who cannot get phone numbers correct and then hangs up.

Slowly, I begin to pick up the pieces. There are moments of temptation. Like one morning when my boss surprises me. He is a nice man. Fifty plus and looking none the worse for it. As I leave his office after an assignment he calls me back.

'Liz, how are you?'

'Fine, Sir.'

'Are you sure you are fine?'

'I am sure, sir.'

'Liz, people talk you know.' Pause. 'I wonder why a man would want to get another wife when he has a gracious, beautiful one like you. Some men have no eyes,' he adds softly.

I cannot maintain the interlock of our eyes. I drop mine.

'Your husband. He must be the biggest fool under the sun.'

I have sworn not to discuss Ishaka negatively with people who are not close to me. He is a buffoon, but he is the man with whom I have lived for the better part of my life. There is no way I will insult him without making a mockery of myself. If I married a buffoon then maybe I cannot be anything else.

'He is fine. The fault is probably mine.'

He shakes his head vehemently.

'No,' he whispers with feeling; the sound of a man struggling to keep his desire to himself. Then he takes me by surprise.

'Liz, give yourself a chance to live again. Get a sparkle in your eyes.'

And before I know it, he grabs me and plants a kiss on my lips.

Under normal circumstance, I would have bitten his lips off and placed them on his table with as much dignity as one can possibly muster in the circumstances. For good measure I would also have brought them on a plate, along with salt, a bottle of ketchup and chilli sauce.

But I know he does not want to take advantage of me. He genuinely cares. I have caught him giving me the *eye* on more than one occasion.

I push him away gently.

'No, please, Sir.'

But I damn near fall for him, *damn* near. Well *somehow*.

He understands. He doesn't trouble me again. But each time he looks at me, there is this sad, longing look in his eyes...

* * *

After a few weeks, he calls me up and tells me to take one month's leave.

'Liz, try to take time off and relax.'

I keep quiet.

'I once cautioned a friend of mine who loves the bottle, that he was living out a cliff-edge existence; that anything could happen and one of these days, he would find herself before his creator,' he continues.

'Forget it Jim,' he answered promptly. 'Let me eat and swig while I still can, before those dismal days catch up with me, when I won't be able to do either. A time will come for all of us when you are so sick and they will ask: 'has the patient taken anything today?' and someone will answer, 'he took a *teaspoon* of Ribena and managed *two* or *three grains* of rice'. Let me take off time to enjoy myself when I still can.'

'I did not argue with him. Liz, let me take you through a personal experience. Two years ago I lay in a hospital, like a child, unable to do anything for myself. I had to be bathed, fed and dressed. I whiled the time away on my back, staring hard at the ceiling, doing nothing else, as some other people did all my work, both personal and official.

'That taught me that the world would not end just because one has taken a break from routine and duty.

'The world will march on anyway, with or without you as an individual. So there is really no harm taking a break and taking time to live, as in living; just being. Amidst the rush all around us, we need to pause for reflection, to think again about life.

'Of course as human beings we each have our weak points. One of those is that we feel good being busy.

'The men take pride in telling people they are so busy they never get enough sleep or they have no time for their families. They feel good as they hop from car to office, from one meeting to another; never pausing on the way to answer a phone call, but moving briskly in a businesslike manner, sometimes calculated to impress everybody who can see them, that they are very, *very* busy.

'Same for the working women, clicking their heels down the corridor, dashing off before answering half the question, moving from home to office, to salon to the women's something club and then ending up home late and tired.

'The housewives will dash from one room to another, first sweeping, then mopping, then cooking, then washing, ironing, eating, talking, visiting, shopping and so on. Some will also take off time minding the neighbours' business for them, getting to know what they ate for supper, when they last ate meat (especially the village folk) or slaughtered chicken and why the wife next door was wailing so loud – though I think that's what good neighbours should do – and whose daughter the bachelor on the next block returned with last night.

'In the final analysis, none of us takes time off to rest.

'Instead of taking a break to rest from the worry and care this hectic world affords us, we are so restless, hopping up and down, home to work, from one taxi to another, all over town, to our friends, enemies and relatives.

'As a result, some people have a perpetual frown on their faces that makes you think Charles Darwin had a point when he said we are descended from apes.

'That is why others develop high blood pressure, others get ulcers while some lose weight inexplicably, or worse still get weakened hearts that can't pump blood straight two days in a row.

'We simply need some time off for ourselves in the midst of this mad rush. It is important to work, but the fact is we can never finish work. As soon as you finish sweeping the room, you will discover some dust is the other corner. Then you want to do away with it too. Then as you mop you discover there is some patch looking funny in this corner, so you go back. Then the kids come trooping in and within moments all you so meticulously accomplished has been undone.

'There will always be work to do, so if your target is to get the work done, then you will work till you drop. Dead. Maybe not now, but for sure later. Why else do you think people just collapse and die without apparent explanation?

'Even the Lord Jesus took off time to be alone. He would abandon the crowds at the end of the 'crusade', move off with His disciples to some quiet place and then leave the disciples and go off by Himself to meditate.

'If He was able to make prudent decisions, maintain a calm exterior and put forward sober answers, it is also because He took off time to confer with His thought apparatus.

'We too need time off, tine to ourselves and time for ourselves.

'Just get some quiet and get mentally refreshed. I assure you Liz, you will find it is healthy and necessary; refreshing and rewarding.

‘Think the world will come to a standstill just because you are away from normal routine, Liz? Wait till you are too ill to do anything (please don’t wait until then!). It will march on like you never existed. So, Liz, go home and relax,’ he ends almost in a whisper.

* * *

As time goes on, I get used to my new life. The cynics who look at me like I have stoned Jesus Christ on the throat soon cease to do so. My natal family who were outraged that I called it quits also fall quiet. They had taken it bad, they really had.

‘How can you ashame the family like this? A woman dies at the cooking stones. At the frontline. You have brought untold humiliation to the family,’ my father had stormed.

‘Father, you are not thinking of the family!’

‘A right thinking person thinks of beyond himself. Thinking about yourself and not the impact your selfish separation will have on the entire family means you are really bad.’ He pauses to get his breath back.

‘And daughter, the fact that Ishaka got another woman, it does not mean that he does not care about you, the first one. Besides, in our language, there is no word to describe infidelity. In Africa, a man can never be unfaithful; he can only be a man.’

‘Well, me I can never understand that.’

‘That’s the whole problem we have now. It is a lost cause.’

But my brother Justus is very supportive. He comes to my new-found home, loaded with chicken and champagne.

‘Liz girl, you are great. Girl am I happy you bullshitted that idiot! You are a woman after my own heart. I hate women who stay in cruel marriages because of all sort of reasons. And yours *was* a cruel marriage... at least psychologically and all the stuff you never told us and which, I am sure, you have no intention of telling us. That Ishaka moron, he humiliated you to the limit. To put another woman on top of you! Liz, your moving away calls for a celebration. If I were loaded, I would have lifted the entire Shoprite here.'

Shoprite is a huge supermarket in town.

Meanwhile a truck is hooting outside the gate; its horn loud enough to make a dead body mumble and stir in its eternal sleep.

The H.B. – not one for the best of public relations - opens the gate to admit whoever it is. Fina, clad in a suit that looks good on her and must have cost quite a few coins, enters, heels clicking with urgency. Anyway, Fina would look gorgeous even in a sack.

'Liz,' she begins as she hugs me. 'We are having a goat-roasting party tonight. You have shown the way forward for women in tortured marriages. Bring the glasses.'

She pops the champagne and with a true modern woman's sense of occasion, pours it in both glasses ceremoniously.

'Here's to a new life after Ishaka. Cheers.' The glasses knock with a clink, before being lifted to the lips.

'Liz, remember: when you flee the devil, make sure you do not leave a forwarding address.' That is material I am sure she plucked straight and unedited out of some book or whatever.

'Ishaka should pay for having killed the sparkle in your eye,' she continues, downing the contents of the glass and proceeding to refill it immediately.

* * *

God! How time runs! Its already one year after I left Ishaka. After office, I decide to go for sauna at the nearest health club. I reach the club, go to the bathroom , remove my clothes and wrap a *kanga* round myself.

'Where is the women's sauna ?' I ask the receptionist.

'Both men and women use the same place,' she says.

Hmm. Anyway I proceed there. Then I find these men and women literally naked. I'm sure the men are involved in oggling at the women rather than enjoying the sauna.

'I cannot sit in with those men,' I tell the receptionist after walking away from the unisex sauna.

She laughs.

'Madam you must be from a nunnery. Other people don't mind. But if you want to go in alone, its fine as long as you pay for all the space.'

I ask her how much it costs. She tells me and luckily, I have the money. But I quickly add that if women customers come, they can pay and join me.

'Who is this that is bringing primitive gender discrimination to our club?' A deep male voice asks.

I turn and look at Arnold.

'I knew it had to be you. The last of the puritans!' Says Arnold.

We both laugh.

'I never pretended to be one.'

'Anyway Liz, long time. But nice to see you.'

'Same here.'

'Liz, am asking for permission. Can I come in and sit in your sauna?'

I laugh.

'Actually Arnold, I have given up the sauna thing. I should not deprive other people of the facility. I will go look for where they have different space for the sexes.'

'Why don't we go do aerobics for today and you look for your club tomorrow?'

'Fine.'

Arnold and I were at campus together and he was good friends with my brother Justus.

As we ride the bicycle and all that sort of thing, we chew the cud. About nothing in particular. Sometimes a lot of nonsense like he asks me whether what he is seeing in the sky is the moon and I tell him not to ask me because I am a stranger in these parts. And we laugh. Sometimes it is good to be able to talk nonsense with somebody. By the end of the exercises, we are cordial.

'See you tomorrow same time Liz?' he asks as he flashes me this million dollar smile that reveals a set of great teeth.

'The pleasure will be mine.'

Arnold. Very pleasant fellow. And very intelligent and knowledgable.

We meet at the club for a week. Then he offers me a drink one evening.

'I will have a glass of wine thanks.'

'Is that what you want or are you just being a lady?'

We both laugh.

'You never know, this wine might just be an introduction to better things to come.' I say playfully.

I have a great evening and by the time I go home, I don't know whether it is the wine or Arnold's company that does it: but I'm feeling so happy, and a bit confused. This feeling is compounded when the phone rings at midnight.

'I just called to say goodnight.' Its Arnold's deep voice.

Goodnight! For me, it is the end of anything called sleep! I am back to the situation of sheep counting! In this particular case I don't want to bring in the vision of my mother, especially when I am thinking naughty.

When the phone rings early in the morning, I jump at it breathless like a marathon runner.

'Yes?'

'Liz, let us meet at the Sheraton at 1.00. Room 16. See you then.'

'See you Arnold,' I say quietly as I replace the receiver. Slowly, I move towards the bathroom. I spend an hour in the bathtub, thinking. I *know* what I am going to the Sheraton for and for sure I am not going to play snakes and ladders with Arnold. We are going for games far more serious. No regrets ... I am not a saint, for God's sake!

The doorknob turns at my discreet knock.

'Arnold, you must have been waiting behind he door!' And we both laugh.

He silences my mouth with a demanding, probing kiss and I find myself responding with the same passion.

'Arnold, you have made me live again after five years. Thank you.' I whisper, after fantastic love making.

'Well, you were a dormant volcano. But I'm happy I have made you happy.'

The following day, I am singing all over the house. The H.G. presents her usual shopping list and I approve of everything. Usually, I would slash most of the items. Kirabo puts in a request for some crazy T-shirts and I give him the money. He hugs me.

The whole day, I wait for Arnold's call but it doesn't come. Neither does he call that night. By morning, I'm a jumble of nerves.

'Arnold what happened?' I ask him on phone.

'Where?' His voice is *normal*!

'You did not call me.'

'Was anything wrong?' He sounds *genuine*!

'Well-er-no. But I expected you to call and say how are you or I love you.'

He laughs.

'Well but of course I do. I mean love you. Why state the obvious?'

'So are we meeting tonight?'

'I'm a bit busy. Lets say over the weekend.'

He keeps his word. And we have another glorious encounter. He does not call me for four whole days after that. I call him.

'Arnold, what *is* happening?'

'Where again?' He asks, again genuinely puzzled.

'Well when are we meeting?'

Then he sounds irritated.

'Look here Liz, what is your problem? We have had fun. I am a married man. You are separated but you have children. Both of us are mature. Now we have had fun. What else do you want?'

I can't believe it. I can't! I read him clearly. And once again in my life, a truth hits me:

In a situation like mine, men want to have fun, women want a relationship. And for me, I am not the type to have fun. Fun my arse!

Slowly, I erase Arnold from my emotional diary. I know it will take time before he gets out of my system, because I had really fallen for him. But time will heal my wounded heart. I meet him occasionally and he is like nothing happened and we are just good friends. I cut out the health club. And I decide not to accept any more of his 'fun' advances.

After three months, he starts looking for me, apologising and all and saying what a heel he is. He begs and begs me to resume the 'affair' with him. But I stick to my resolve. Funny. When I wanted him, all he was in for was fun. Now when I have erased him, he wants a fully fledged affair...

I know I will find love. Thing to do is keep the door to my heart open. And somebody nice is welcome; somebody who really cares, not some silly and despicable sucker.

CHAPTER SEVEN

THE RETURN OF THE NATIVE

The phone rings. Good thing with these mobile phones, you look at it and decide whether to speak or not to. You either know the caller or you don't.

'Yes, Fina?'

'Liz, how're things?'

'Could be better but I am not complaining. What's the latest?'

'I don't know whether it is good or bad news, but Ishaka is sick.'

'Of course it *is* bad news, Fina. You should know me better than that. What's it?'

'From what I have gathered, its not the plague.' AIDS.

But even if it were, now AIDS is not a death sentence like it was in the past when there was absolutely no remedy. To date, many people with it thank medical science. There are drugs that make it like one can live with high blood pressure or diabetes. Though of course most of these drugs are unaffordable for most of our people. But that power called hope keeps all of us optimistic that the price will soon be drastically reduced.

So a person like Ishaka is able to afford the drugs. That is if he is HIV positive. I don't know when this thing will go away from us. I mean the minute you hear somebody is sick, most people jump to the conclusion that it must be AIDS. As if there are no other diseases. God, how I hate that attitude.

It just sends me raving mad.

'So what is ailing Ishaka?'

'I am not very sure. But I will find out.'

'Keep me informed. I hope he gets better soon.'

'I hope not.'

'Fina!'

'Not soon anyway.'

'Fina!'

She laughs with cruelty.

Apparently the news is not good. Ishaka has some complicated condition. And that Manga has been hiding him from people! *Mbu* she did not want people seeing how thin he is. Then they would spread rumours that he has AIDS. How primitive!

'Fina, just tell whoever is close to Ishaka to take him to hospital.'

'The woman insists that he gets home care.'

The situation deteriorates, so Fina tells me. Then I am preparing to go and see Ishaka when a car hoots at my gate. The shamba boy opens.

'Madam, it is a special hire. It has brought an old man. Maybe your father, Madam,' the shamba boy says.

Maybe your father, Madam! When I go to the car, I get the shock of my life! My *father* is none other than Ishaka!

'Ishaka!'

'Yes it is me. Please help me out,' he whispers almost inaudibly.

I get hold of his emaciated arm, the size of a vein in a healthier body; hold around the waist which if I hadn't seen before would have said was given to him when the creator was in a particularly miserly mood and we crawl to the sitting room.

He collapses on the sofa as sweat runs down his face and he gasps for breath like a fish that has been swept out of the sea and onto the shore.

'Water,' he whispers, with the strength a dying fish, desperate for air.

I quickly get it and he holds out his hand like a starving man grabbing the last available morsels of food.

His hand shakes uncontrollably as he passes it over his mouth. He tries to speak but only blubbers incoherently like a baboon that has caught sight of a snake but just can't mouth the words to express its feelings.

'Ishaka, take it easy. Just lie back. Don't try to say anything. Regain your breath first.'

He stares at me. A film of tears covers his eyes.

Okay, Fina has told me about his sickness. But this is something beyond what I expected. He is exhausted the poor thing. He falls into this sleep that keeps breaking up as he groans. I sit beside him until I realise that I should call a doctor.

'Well, bring him to the hospital. I cannot treat him by remote control for heaven's sake!' The doctor says or rather barks at me.

I prepare myself for another less-than-enthusing encounter with the chaps who spend six years at school – double the average gestation period for a bachelor's degree – only to come out and sometimes issue reports that conflict and contradict, punctuated with huge medical terms, with intent to confuse us the poor ignoramuses.

Go to one and he tells you that you have malaria 'plus, plus'. He gives you a detailed prescription two pages long and by the time you are through with the pharmacist you will require the services of a small truck to carry the medicine home. The more creative patient might want to start a small pharmacy with this lot, with a view to making a quick profit.

The next doctor says no way; this is a simple case of very scanty malaria. Take this (a couple of anti-malaria tablets and some concoction in a bottle) and you'll be fine by this time tomorrow.

The third doctor takes one look at you and promptly pronounces rheumatic fever. When she first heard 'rheumatic fever' a friend of mine got it all wrong and understood 'romantic fever' instead. Since she was processing her divorce papers, she momentarily thought the doctor was spot on.

* * *

I decide not to wake up Ishaka. He doesn't sleep much though.

'Ishaka, I am taking you to hospital.'

He agrees meekly, knowing it won't make sense to argue and he does not even have the energy to resist. Meanwhile, a foul smell assails the air as, perplexed, I look at him and as my hands slowly find their way to my nose.

'Maybe the sewer has burst,' I say apologetically.

Strange though. It hasn't happened ever since I have been here.

'I'm sorry Liz. I cannot hold my diarrhoea,' he says as tears of frustration flood his eyes. Oh God!

'That's okay. Just a minute.'

I dash to the bathroom. To tell you the truth, I wouldn't ordinarily relish cleaning the shit off a mature person. But Ishaka cannot take himself to the toilet and besides, this is the man who took me from my parents' home. It's not his fault anyway that he is sick. I cannot tell the H.G. to do it. So I proceed to the bathroom and pull out a pair of gloves. The ones that come with the hair dye. I put them on and proceed to the sitting room. I unzip Ishaka's trousers and pull them down.

'I'm sorry Liz,' he repeats.

Well, I would not be being exactly honest if I tell him 'its alright.' The usual crap even when you know it isn't. But I will clean him all the same.

'Ishaka, you are not well. So please forget about feeling bad.'

And I proceed to clean him. After which I get one of the trousers Justus left behind.

'Liz, she threw me out. Said there is no way she can clean away the shit of a mature person. Then there was no way I could call anybody to my rescue because I was scared about their reaction. Until this morning after she had left the house and told me she did not want to find me still hanging around (except maybe on a rope) when she returns from work. She put my clothes in a suitcase and threw it outside.

'I closed my eyes, swallowed my pride and called the houseboy. I asked him to wash me. This is his pair of trousers,' he laughs weakly, apologetically. 'I told him, the houseboy, to get me a taxi, which he did,' that weak apologetic smile again, 'and here I am.'

'Let's go.'

I support him as we struggle to my car.

He is admitted as soon as we reach the hospital.

For weeks, he floats between life and death. I tell Eva and Kirabo as gently as I can and take her to hospital one day.

'Daddy?' She screams with pleasure. 'You look all screwed up now.'

'Eva! That's terrible language! Stop it.'

But what do I expect? Our people say that when you steal with your child strapped on your back, the child perfects the art.

'Sorry Mom. Dad, I was saying you look like Rip Van Winkle but you *are* Daddy.'

She has read all about Rip Van Winkle, the man who slept for twenty years and woke up to find the rest of the world had moved on while he slept. More importantly, he himself was precisely where he was twenty years before; no progress. Just vegetating; rooted to the same spot and remaining in the same economic ranks as before while everybody else is marching on.

Even though Eva is unaware of this deeper analysis of her father's disposition, I am startled that she could be so inadvertently right on.

'But it sure is nice to see you.'

Then she pauses for effect and then shouts at the top of her lungs:

'Daddy, I want a diskman YESTERDAY!'

Kirabo and I laugh; her father only manages a weak and tired smile as she glares at us like we are the biggest idiots ever to traverse the earth.

During one of those days, Fina also comes.

'Liz, you know what, you are a living saint and I have a mind to look for the Pope to canonise you immediately."

'Fina, kindly spare me your cynicism. Keep it for the buffoons in your village bar.'

After the hustle of the last few weeks, I am not exactly in charitable mood just now and will brook no small talk.

'Look, damn it! A man abandons you for another woman…'

'No, he did not. It's just that I couldn't stand the relationship where you share a husband. I am the one who left him, remember? We must be true to history.'

'Please don't give me that bullshit. He is the one who practically left you. Now look who is defending who.' She is actually annoyed. But I think I also know who has enriched Eva's hostile vocabulary in recent times.

'Thing is not to apportion blame *now*. I mean we don't even have to talk about who left who. It is neither here nor there. Look, Ishaka is sick enough for two.'

'You are telling me! Look, Liz. Every dog has its day; and it is clear this one's has finally arrived. A little overdue if I may delve into the uncharitable for now, but just in time to give him his share of misery that he thought he would never come across.'

'Fina!'

'Yeeees,' she digs in with more cruelty. 'Knowing Ishaka, I am sure he did not come across this misery. It waited too long for him to show up and when he didn't, probably chose to go looking for him instead. And by the look of things, he has been amply compensated for all the misery he missed out in years gone by.'

'Fina! How can you be so cruel?'

'I am only stating a fact. All I am saying is this guy abandons you and flies into the arms of some idiot. Then he falls sick. Hard luck. She turns him out. He flies back to you like nothing happened. I mean this man has crashed worse than a computer. Not because of his illness but because his lady has thrown him out. He has no job, no source of income. When they crash they always come crawling back – the worms.

'I pray he recovers. He will. Suppose he wants to stay with you for keeps, will you accept?'

I keep quiet.

'Well, will you?' She persists.

I still don't answer.

'Liz, silence means consent you know.'

And then I blow all my fuses.

'Look here, Fina. Leave me alone. I mean the way you are carrying on it is as if I am on trial, for God's sake! Silence means consent, indeed! You are sounding like those goddam judges. And yet you flunked your first year in law school...'

'At least I *sat* for the examination anyway. And even though I failed, I repeated and passed well,' she says between her teeth. 'Maybe it is now time to talk about *those* who passed examinations they did *not* sit for.'

'You know that is not true,' I protest. 'That is a story concocted by that lecturer whose approaches I rejected.'

'Hmm! Tell that to the birds. Now I understand why Ishaka got Manga,' she retorts.

'At least I got somebody to propose and marry me. I know *someone* who has not even been asked out as a joke, forget about being proposed to. I also know that she is still floating around like a leaf in the wind and uses the women's lib as an excuse for her failure to get a man.'

'Look at you,' she says with a truckload of contempt. 'You were more or less a widow, even as your so-called husband lived. I detest and despise your type, keeping up appearances for the benefit of the company you are in;

'Oh, I must rush home and roast some goat ribs for my husband.' 'Oh, I must run and give him company because he will fret and fuss if he finds me away.' 'Oh, my husband cannot eat without me.' All bull... Talking for the gallery yet you know your husband will not be there to eat whatever it is you are preparing. I'd rather stay alone than pretend to be married.'

'You know Liz,' she continues, wagging a finger and almost poking it into my eyes. 'You wasted your education; you are just an educated illiterate.'

That is the ultimate blow and it hits me below the belt. I bow my head and ask myself, what are we doing to each other?

'I'm sorry, Fina,' I begin, regretting my outburst. 'It's just that the events of these few weeks are taking their toll on me. But I also think it is the wrong timing for you to ask me questions like if Ishaka recovers and wants to come back...I mean for me right now, the only thing I care about is for him to get well.'

'I'm sorry too. Guess I got overzealous,' she says as we embrace.

* * *

Ishaka has been in hospital for one month that was certainly longer than a year, from my point of view; and this bright sunny morning the doctor comes and says he is now okay and discharges him.

Not a bad way to begin the day, I think.

Ishaka looks at me and smiles in humility. A humility last seen when he asked my father for my hand in marriage.

'Liz, I owe my life to you...' he begins.

He looks down like he is counting his fingers, lost for words; like a woman absorbing every word of the man making advances to her and harbouring the intention to say yes but not sure how to bring it out.

I have not forgotten that look on his face. It is *deja-vu*...those early times when he used to court me.

'Liz,' Ishaka looks up, 'thank you for everything...I... I... I... do not know how to express my gratitude.'

'I know I hurt you real bad and do not even deserve the forgiveness I ask. But please forgive me. Give me one last chance; come back to me. Be my wife again.'

It is like he is popping the question again.

'Ishaka, please don't thank me, I just did my duty.'

I pause for a minute or two, pondering…no, looking for my next statement.

'And about coming back to you…'

I am more than relieved when my mobile phone rings. I hurriedly get it before the first ring finalises – this is no time to engage in an issue that will change my life all over again. And certainly not enough time to compose an appropriate answer.

'Hello,' I say into to the mouthpiece. It is Fina. I am more than glad for the diversion. Life promptly gets a lot easier.

'Fina, I have good news for you. Ishaka has been discharged...yes...yes…not to worry…I will tell him…okay…okay….yes…okay…Do me a favour will you, pass by my office and ask Mr. Kimeta to give you the office car so that we can take Ishaka…okay...we will discuss that when you are here…I appreciate that thought…see you in fifteen minutes.'

Fina finds me packing Ishaka's things. She greets us in this voice that could turn water to ice in a moment.

Together we put Ishaka's cargo into the car and go back to the room to get him.

We walk together to the car. Ishaka is bouncing about the place with the air of a man who has just purchased the premises.

Clearly he is in high spirits, like a novice lawyer who has won his first case in court and would like to recount every detail to whomsoever will listen.

Fina sits in the passenger seat while Ishaka relaxes in the back seat.

As the car eases out of the hospital's large iron grilled gate, the driver caresses the brakes and asks, 'Where are we going?'

Then there is this nine months pregnant silence during which time stands still. Nobody moves.

Ishaka pioneers the break up of the inertia. He turns slowly, like a ship docking in deep waters and looks at me with a steady gaze, like a lawyer about to begin a brawling cross-examination.

Fina makes a ninety degrees turn of the neck that a flamingo would find exciting as she looks at me – her eyes speaking volumes.

The driver cranes his neck with the grace of a pickpocket checking to see what is in his quarry's pocket and looks in the rear view mirror, trying to get an answer from me.

After what seems like eternity, Fina breaks the silence and says:

'Liz, you know where you are *not* going!'

"What do you mean?" I ask trying to look as innocent as a toddler.

'Liz,' Fina dictates. "We are dropping Ishaka at his house and then we are taking you to *your* house!'

'Fina, with all due respect to you, you will not become the destiny to my body, soul, and spirit!'

Fina jumps out of the car and marches to my door. The driver turns off the ignition key to save fuel, I think or to hear the exchange better, awaiting some juicy gossip.

'Liz, this man...' her eyes raging with anger and an ugly sneer to her twitched lips continues with a sideway *thumbs-up* pointing to Ishaka, '...left you for another woman! You put so much in his life, business, and emotional stability. You would give him advice. When you had the strength to leave him eventually, you hang on to your marital name, *his name...*'

At this juncture she flares up better than a fireworks display on New Year's Day '...giving a bad name to the Women's Lib!'

Now she is stammering and the saliva flies out of her mouth like shells from a stealth bomber that urgently needs hushkitting.

'If you had two hours, I would mention everything this despicable man has done to you. This man thinks with his *dick*.'

Fina literary spits on the tarmac. The sound is a loud *'kapoot'*. I am not sure her spittle made the tarmac crack, but with that sound I can't rule it out.

'I can see that you are set to have this louse back!'

Fina laughs. A dry laugh reminiscent of twigs set on fire.

'Let me tell you, Liz, beware; a man like Ishaka is deceitful above all things. He will break a promise or breach a contract with ease. A man is a man at five o'clock!' Fina is still firm in her convictions about the integrity of men – or to be precise, the lack of it.

'Five a.m. or five p.m.?' I ask.

'Take it like that.'

'Like what?'

'Like that.'

I hate it when people talk that way. Take it like that indeed!

She is not yet done. 'The official wife sticks through *sick* and *sin* eh? How touching and noble!'

She bangs the car door shut, from the outside and storms off, stomping her feet in protest like a child who has just learnt that her mother has for the second time in two days, returned home without any ice cream.

As her short footsteps fade away I realise that for the first time in so many years, Fina will travel by public means. I hope she still knows how to stop a taxi. Or that she can recognise a bus when she comes across one.

* * *

Even though I admit Fina has a point, I know things are not as easy as she makes them sound. I won't throw out Ishaka, my husband of many years and father to my children (is there an end to his credentials in my life?) just because some member of the women's lib – best friend though she be – thinks I should.

I have a good job, so Ishaka doesn't have to play my Santa Claus. But so what; did I marry Ishaka to earn a living?

Will the money and furniture talk to me?

I need intimate communication and I will not feed the social mirror satisfaction like Fina wants me to. And anyway, aren't all families dysfunctional since the beginning of sin?

But more importantly, I am not the only player in this whole thing; there is more than me in this equation.

'Madam, where are we going?'

The driver's voice – a shrill and comical affair that reminds me of a cockerel learning how to crow – brings me back to the present.

'Drive to Mr. Ishaka's house.' My voice is firm and unequivocal.

Ishaka's face twists into a huge ball of surprise – I suddenly realise how fast he has aged since I left him – then breaks into a huge grin as his hands, now much stronger, wrap around me in a huge embrace.

The hug lasts much longer than intended and is only broken when I feel a wetness on my shoulders.

Can it be? I ask myself silently as I release him and bring his face forward.

It is my turn to be surprised: Ishaka's eyes are wet with tears! For the first time ever since I married him I see Ishaka shedding tears.

As he smiles through his tears I am relieved to see that these are tears of relief and joy that accompany a long-awaited homecoming. I instinctively know the cock that had found a new nest by the brook has finally come home to roost. Mercifully he had not brought Manga to our house; so the place, a few stains notwithstanding, had not been desecrated.

I pick up the phone and dial Fina's number. It rings for sometime and just when I am about to give up she answers with a curt 'hello?'.

'Fina, I am so sorry.'

'About what?'

'Everything. My bad behaviour. I didn't treat you too nice last time.

'Look Fina; I know you care for me. You really do. It's just that I'll have to sit with you and explain this thing.'

Silence on the other side.

'You know Liz,' she begins after what seems a real long while, ever since that louse Ishaka started misbehaving you thought you could change him; make him turn around. That was of course, not possible. Like the Good Book asks, can the leopard change his spots or the Ethiopian his skin?

'Now the bastard comes crawling back like the worm he is, and you accept him like you had sent him away yourself on some little vacation supposed to work for your own good.

'Take it from me, Liz. As soon as Ishaka is back on his feet and working; and as soon as the money starts rolling in, he will waddle back to Manga and she will accept him back.

'Fina…'

'Liz, it's your life. I hope I'll be around when that man abandons you a second time. When they do it the first time and get away with it, they will always try it out again. I will grind his fucking balls and send the powder to him in a beautiful envelope.

'This is not a threat; it is a promise,' Fina says in low, carefully measured tones. The line goes dead.

She is a great friend, is Fina. She speaks her mind and sees no need to embellish what she deems dangerous.

Next I dial Eva.

'We are having dinner tonight in the big house with daddy.'

Eva screams with the pleasure of a cat that has chanced upon a bowl of cream. I listen to the screams a moment more and switch off the phone, a smile on my lips…but maybe not as big as Ishaka's. The smile I mean.

'May I borrow your phone?' The experience has evidently taught Ishaka some manners as well. Politeness just had never been his way of doing things. I oblige.

'What is Kirabo's number?' There is apology written all over the request. This is a much humbler, fairly subdued and completely sober version of Ishaka. He is sorry – almost embarrassed – that he did not have his son's number.

'Hello.' A calm voice is in charge of the phone this time. None of the arrogant 'where are you?' we've been used to.

'Son, this is daddy.'

There is probably silence on the other end, for Ishaka once again ventures, 'yes Kirabo; it *is* your dad. Look son, tomorrow I want us to fix that broken pipe that we never finished working on, in the kitchen.'

This is too good to be true. I close my eyes and offer a prayer of thanks to Jesus; far more sincere a prayer than I had ever offered before.

There are broken pipes all over my life; wounds, scars and pains all over. The broken pipes in the family will take a while to mend. But at least I can see the process has began; and for that I am thankful.